MW00615044

THE FIRST WIFE'S TALE

THE FIRST WIFE'S TALE

A MYSTERY

BY

J N CATANACH

THE HORNBILL PRESS

NEW YORK
2020

Published by The Hornbill Press, New York
thehornbillpress@gmail.com
First Edition. Text set in Georgia 12 pt
Printed in the United States of America by KDP,
an amazon.com company
Author photo © by Marion Ettlinger

Library of Congress Control Number: 2019955669
ISBN: 978-0-9706407-7-2

For first wives everywhere

CHAPTER ONE

Detective sergeant Flora MacFaddin of the Toronto Metropolitan Police Homicide and Missing Persons Division, was having a very good day. For nearly eleven years, virtually single-handedly and long after the detectives originally assigned to the case had retired, she had kept the Kristi Aranda murder out of the unsolved file. From almost the beginning, the detective had had a suspect in her sights. But without solid evidence she knew there was no way in the world she could touch him. Today the evidence had walked in the door. And it fitted beautifully her theory.

Holding a photograph in her left hand—the life-size side view of a woman's bare neck, slender and fair as in a pastel portrait—with her gloved right hand she picked up a man's silk scarf. Attached to the scarf by its wire stem was a faded red poppy, the metal pistil of which she gently pressed into a point on the photo just below the ear, a dark area about a pencil-width across.

Even without the blonde hairs caught in the wire—one of which was presently with Forensics—MacFaddin was convinced she had a fit. Here, she told herself, was the murder weapon. And feeling the soft sheen of the fabric, it seemed to her that the suspicion that had nagged at her all these years was vindicated. This was not the garb of some down and out prowler, this was the adornment of a man of wealth and taste.

On the self-same stifling summer day that found Detective sergeant MacFaddin poring over evidence in her Toronto office, some five hundred miles away to the south-east, Annette Warrender was taking a call in her Manhattan co-op.

She stood very still, her hand on the phone. By lifting her hand she could break the connection between her palm and the shiny plastic of the receiver she'd just replaced. And she didn't want to do that. Not right away. She closed her eyes. She needed time to think. A metallic squeak from the hall startled her. The maid had dragged the vacuum cleaner into the doorway where she waited, poised between anticipation and incomprehension.

"Oh, Mrs Wing," the connection was broken, "yes, I'm through. Sorry. I was on the phone. Please go ahead with the bedroom."

Mrs Wing shot her employer an odd, sly, attentive look. She hadn't understood a word. Americans were so unpredictable. Having spent most of her three score years in a village near Shanghai, she was still getting the hang of life in New York where her daughter had come to live after the troubles.

"Bed-room," Annette enunciated, cradling her hands against her cheek and closing her eyes. Soon the drone of the machine filled the apartment.

Poor Mrs Wing. Annette blushed to think about it. First yelling and gesticulating at her over the din, then yanking the plug out of the wall and running back here to the phone as if she was sliding into home base. The name—that's what did it—the man's voice and then the name suddenly like that, out of nowhere. Not, 'This is Roy Warrender,' as she thought she heard (before disabling the vacuum cleaner) but obviously, in retrospect, a question: 'Mrs Roy Warrender?'

He'd sounded reasonable, the man. A lawyer he said he was. Yes, she had been Mrs Roy Warrender, she conceded, though a while ago. Perhaps there were other, more recent, claimants. A note of wariness must have crept into her voice because the man was quickly at pains to soothe. The only Warrender in the Manhattan book. A great liberty. Nothing at all to be alarmed about, just a spot of legal housecleaning (had he chuckled?), and did the name Annette Shaheen Warrender mean anything to her?

Well yes, she'd said, that's me.

The matter was such—direct quote—that it could not be satisfactorily disposed of on the phone. The man would be glad to call round in person at any convenient time, that very morning if it suited. Which made Annette even more wary. Since when in New York did lawyers make house calls? Was there something to sign? Some elaborate con under way? And if Roy was involved, all the more reason to be on her guard. Hadn't Colin warned her of exactly this: that some day Roy would come back to haunt her. So call Colin. Ask his advice. And have him snap at her in his run-along-and-play British way? 'Annie darling, you are the world's absolutely number one ninnypoop.' Or words to that effect. No, better find out first what it was all about. A meeting was arranged for early that afternoon. He would send a car.

All through Mrs Wings's English lesson—a half hour tacked on to her morning's cleaning—Annette's mind wandered. And Mrs Wing kept staring at her in a speculative manner. Was she losing her grip? If she was honest, she knew her time with Colin was running out, and with it any firm belief in herself. "Lemmie," she struggled to explain, "is slang for 'let me.' Let me go, let me do it,' and so on. Slang? That's a sort of lazy English. Lazy? Not doing any work. Like me? Mrs Wing! I may be lazy, but I'm not slang." Perhaps *Huckleberry Finn* hadn't been the best choice after all.

The reception area of the lawyer's midtown office was unexpectedly plush with floor to ceiling views down the length of Manhattan. Because of old memories of Roy—perhaps unfair to a man she'd not set eyes on in twenty years—she'd anticipated something more workaday, worn carpets and a lingering stench of cigar. Well, maybe Roy had come up in the world. He'd always threatened to.

"Mrs Warrender?"

She turned to see a small, balding man in a pink shirt and green bow tie. Wielding a pair of tortoiseshell spectacles he herded her into a corner office that seemed to perch like a hawk's aerie over the fuming city. As soon as she was settled in a comfortable chair, the man—who introduced himself as "Baffle, one of the senior partners"—scuttled behind a desk. Standing with his back to the window, he picked up a slender file. "Roylance Calvin Warrender."

Annette shifted her rear end expectantly on the seat. "Are you aware, Mrs Warrender, that your, er, former husband named you in a Will as sole heir to his estate in the event of his demise?"

"You mean he's *dead*?" She'd hardly expected this.

"You're not in touch?"

"Not since the divorce. I was mad as heck at him when he left."

Baffle's swift glance unsettled her. "In his only extant Will— the only one we've been able to trace—Warrender leaves everything to you. But addressing the specifics of your question, as far as we know the answer is conceivably yes."

Annette groped for a response. Scarcely had she conjured Roy back to life and here he was dead. Not that the news should affect her in any special way. But if the years had sealed up the cracks and numbed the pain, what was this dull, flat feeling that caught her in the pit of the stomach? She was conscious again of the lawyer's gaze, of his wanting something more than she felt it in herself to give. "May I see?" She reached out a hand across the desk.

He walked around and laid a paper in her lap, a standard Will form with a November 1969 date. 'I, Roylance Calvin Warrender,' she read, 'being of sound and disposing mind and memory, and considering the uncertainty of this life, do make, publish and declare this to be my last Will and Testament as follows, hereby revoking all other former Wills by me at any time made. First, after my lawful debts are paid, I give'—here typed in—'all of which I die possessed to my loving wife, Annette Shaheen Warrender.' Then the flashy, once familiar, signature.

"Funny," she said, "I just don't remember this. And these names"—two witnesses had signed under Roy—"mean nothing to me. Nothing."

"But the signature?"

"Oh, that's Roy all right, his executive flourish, I used to call it. Funny though, he had a thing about Wills. A Will was like an invitation to a funeral as far as he was concerned." It was all rushing back to her. "Death to him was a man with a briefcase with a Will inside it; a man knocking on your door at an inopportune moment. Like Dad, he'd say. After he lost the farm, his dad sold things door to door, whatever he could make a buck on. Oh, you know what could have happened? My father settled some money on us and this was something he made Roy do. Shows he had a pretty accurate line on his new son-in-law."

"I'm afraid he did." Baffle moved back behind his desk. "Mrs Warrender, I'll be frank with you. From all appearances you're a woman of means. You live in a nice part of town, you are, if I may say so, expensively and exquisitely turned out. I probably won't ruin your day when I tell you you're not about to inherit the crown jewels. As you've perhaps guessed, the operative sentence is the first."

She glanced down. "After my lawful debts are paid?"

"Surprise you?"

Annette shrugged. "What does surprise me is that I'm sitting here at all. You call me down to tell me I've inherited nothing from someone I've not seen in twenty years. What is this?" She was angry now, not because her hopes had been raised about an inheritance, but that they'd been raised about something else, something she couldn't fully fathom. "What about his nearest and dearest? Why not talk to them? What about his wife ?"

Baffle pounced. "So you knew he'd married again?"

"Yes."

"He told you?"

"They sent me a wedding invitation. I tore it up."

"Mrs Warrender," leaning towards her he splayed his fingers on the desk. "We've done our homework, there is no other Will. The document you see before you was traced to a bank. The First Peoples Bank of Hazardville. That's in Northern Connecticut."

"Where we grew up."

"And as to wives," Baffle glanced speculatively at another file but made no move to pick it up, "at the present time there does not appear to be one."

An unpleasant thought weevilled its way into Annette's mind. "What sort of debt did Roy leave? I mean how much are we talking about?"

Baffle's hand dropped lightly onto a thick folder. He lifted the cover, then shut it quickly. "Upwards of a half-million dollars." Adding, as if in mitigation, "Canadian."

"You're not saying— I mean, I'm not—" A vision of Colin loomed large. Colin in one of his icy rages, surgically reducing her with his scalpel as his students, masked and gowned, thronged the operating theater.

Baffle eyed her over his glasses. Pityingly? Regretfully? She stuttered to a halt. "Mrs Warrender, I'm duty bound to advise you that in no way, shape or form can you, as heir to the estate, be held responsible for debts incurred beyond the means of the estate to pay. In the eyes of the law you are no more related to Roylance Warrender than to the man in the moon. You are not responsible for his obligations."

"Half a million," Annette whistled. Reassured, she groped for explanations. "How did he—? His death, I mean. Was it—?"

"Suicide. Is that what you were going to say?"

She nodded.

"Would it surprise you?"

"I don't know. People change. The Roy I knew, I'd have to say yes. Why? How shall I put it? Because nothing seemed to get to him. The duck's back, that was Roy. I mean imagine, after all he put me through, the guy invites me to his wedding." She laughed. "But then with those debts... *Was* it suicide?"

Baffle lowered his eyes. For the first time he seemed not quite at ease in her presence. "The fact of the matter is we're not quite sure he's dead, not one hundred percent."

"Good God," Annette thrust herself back in her chair. She fixed the lawyer with a look—half pleading, half exasperated. "Well, how dead is he?"

Baffle waggled a plump hand. For a moment or two they observed each other across the desk. Any number of questions rampaged through her mind. Finally, she said, "We. Who's we? Why don't you just lay the whole thing out for me?"

Baffle's head roved back and forth over his files and folders like a metal detector. His lips twitched. "I never met Roy Warrender, but I think I can safely say this: nobody who did came away whole. Not so long ago he was living in considerable splendor in Toronto, Canada. Then he drops out of sight. Early last month his creditors—the principals, banks mainly, are represented in the States by this firm—ran him to ground in Southern Maryland. Some sort of summer colony, I gather. He'd concocted a new identity for himself. As the net closed, he managed to slip away. The trail went cold."

The picture of Roy hunted through the South like an escaped slave—his pursuers baying behind him—Annette found strangely moving. If only she'd been there for him, to sit him down and sort him out, all the things she hadn't been equipped to do for him twenty years ago. It was only the lawyer's sharp eyes that kept hers dry.

"You're not bound to answer this, Mrs Warrender, but I have to ask. Has he, er, in any way contacted you?"

She laughed, incredulous. "I told you, it's been twenty—"

"*Recently?*"

She bristled. "What exactly are you getting at?"

"Don't misunderstand me, Mrs Warrender. You *are* his first wife, remember."

"So?"

"I've been in this business a long time. It's amazing the way a man in trouble—real trouble—will turn to the first wife. Don't ask me to explain. I can't. It's just something I've observed." He leaned towards her. "Tell me, Mrs Warrender, what is it about first wives?"

CHAPTER TWO

First wives. First wives.

Annette smoldered on her way home in the back seat of the limousine. What did that smugly-married-seeming little man— she'd seen the ring—know about first wives? First wives bruise easily, have impressionable parts. They are tolerant, thinking life is on their side. They are loyal, bearing in mind the children to come. They yearn for the patina well-married time achieves, and end up with waxy yellow build-up. So much for first wives.

Yet Baffle had a point. Unlikely—but not inconceivable—that Roy, in a really tight spot, might seek her out. Hadn't Colin predicted it? That he'd *not* done so hadn't stopped Annette from leaving open the possibility in the lawyer's mind that he might, or even had. Let him wonder. If Baffle hoped that she—in her innocence—might lead Roy's pursuers to him, that particular street ran two ways. Why, she'd asked him—as long as she was Roy's sole heir—shouldn't she go down to Maryland herself to pick over anything he'd left behind. Baffle, momentarily at a loss, ended up dictating an official-looking letter of introduction to the Calvert County police.

Roy, a suicide? Do people change that much? If he resembled at all the man she'd known, Roy would be very much alive. Roy, single and on the lam. Speeding up the FDR Drive, her heart danced a little gavotte of anticipation. Some live action was precisely what she needed to juice up her hair-and-nail-salon punctuated existence. She was forty-three, supposedly in the prime of life, yet lately had felt as flaccid as August in the city beyond the windows of the air-conditioned limo.

That afternoon at their weekly coffee kvetch Annette looked forward to an audience ready and eager to be titillated and, if at all possible, scandalized. None of her friends, she was certain, would have anything quite as juicy to contribute. By the time the chauffeur let her off at her building, Annette had more or less decided what she was going to do. Later, beating up the ingredients of her famous Lebanese deviled eggs—her grandmother's recipe—she came to a conclusion. Colin: that was the crux of the matter. It was time she stopped trying to kid herself.

Not one of the friends who came that afternoon had met—or even seen—Colin. So long had it been since a get-together had had to be rescheduled because he was in town, that speculation arose as to whether he was still 'in the picture'. All they had to go on was a photo in a leather frame of a lean, soldierly man—perhaps in his mid-forties—in a light-colored suit and open-neck shirt, arms folded, straw hat pulled down over his eyes. A photo taken by Annette on a trip to the Grand Canyon some years ago, a fixture on her living room mantelpiece.

The story of their meeting one rainy night near Lincoln Center was legend. Colin, first to the door of a yellow cab, graciously held it for her. "Why don't we share?" she offered on the spur of the moment, and he folded his lanky frame in after her. Turned out they'd both been at the opera, Annette—though she didn't let on—in the standing section at the back of the Family Circle.

You can joke about anything, but with some things you put at risk more than is safe. And the topic of Colin's increasingly extended absences was one of those things. Too much seemed to ride on it. So when Annette related the story of the lawyer from the moment her phone rang to the moment she walked out of his office, and followed through with some pithy comments having to do with Colin's negligence and what she might just do about it, like become a little negligent herself, she signaled a Jericho-like tumbling down of walls.

In the ensuing merriment, each woman chimed in with her own tale of the 'Negligencia', a species on which they claimed expertise. "We could be famous group," cried Jadwiga, a concert pianist who reputedly in her day dazzled audiences from Havana to Harbin and now sold tickets at a cinema on West 57th Street. "The neglected ones sing songs of hate."

"Just don't leave yourself short," cautioned Winifred, whose chief source of income—as far as anyone could tell—was jury duty. And Josie, a teacher who'd taken early retirement from her job and her husband, counseled, "Go for it!"

It was Winifred who shed some light on the lawyer's suspicious attitude. In the confusion of his call he might be forgiven for getting the impression that Annette was *expecting* a call from Roy. "By the way, is he available?" she asked. "Winifred Baffle has a certain cachet."

Later as she was putting away dishes, Annette flicked on the radio for company. Crystal Gayle was singing, 'I'd do it all over again'. If that wasn't telling her something, she decided, she was deaf. Why, Roy might even find her attractive. The hayseed he'd once known had learned a thing or two, like how to groom herself to maximum effect. Heck, hadn't the lawyer noticed.

Later, as the euphoria of the afternoon wore off, she reconsidered the call to Colin. His advice usually proved sound. She'd grown to count on it. Even the new bedroom drapes were basically his choosing, though he'd not yet set eyes on them and probably wouldn't notice if he walked in tonight. Which was another thing: the sporadic, unannounced arrivals when she was supposed to be here waiting, waiting, waiting. "Just nipped over on Concorde." What did he think she did all day when he wasn't here? "What's cooking, Tiger Pet? Ha ha." And he'd sweep her off to some exclusive eatery. Yes, there were compensations, as she'd remind herself time and again over the years. He'd opened up the world for her, explained it, defined it. Because what did *she* ever know?

It was too late to call the hospital now, and if she tried the flat she might get his wife. It had happened. Twice. She knew, of course—the wife. So why keep up the pretense? It was something to do with being British. There was that time, oh, in the late seventies, Annette went to JFK to meet a nephew of Colin's—some scheduling foul-up—and sitting in the coffee shop between flights and sucks on a milkshake, this seven-year-old looks up at her: "Are you Uncle Colin's little bit on the side?" Oh yes, they knew.

The following morning, Annette donned her leopardskin leotards, brewed a cup of strong coffee and, feeling courageous, put a call through to Colin's office at the hospital—among London's renowned. His secretary—a treasure trove of secrets who managed to sound solicitous no matter what—said that the doctor had just left for India, a maharishi needing an emergency op, and she wasn't sure when he'd be back. Was it urgent? She had a number in Mumbai.

No, said Annette, not really. Thanks. Her next call was to a travel agent.

From Dulles International Airport the highway cut east through the wooded Virginia countryside. Skirting the Washington suburbs, it bridged the Potomac, grazed Andrews Air Force Base and angled south across the rolling peach and tobacco fields of Maryland's Calvert County.

Annette, at the wheel of a rented Caprice, had more the sensation of launching into space than spinning along on mere earthbound tarmac. With sunglasses pushed back on her glistening hair, a sandaled foot nudging the gas pedal and country and western music from a local station blaring quadraphonically in her ears, she was experiencing something missing from her life in a long time: freedom. Her decision to find Roy, alive or dead, arrived at in guilt, rebellion and trepidation back in New York City, seemed now to be not only right but inevitable. Whether or not she succeeded hardly mattered.

Wrenched bodily from the half-life to which only yesterday she'd thought herself condemned, she could imagine no other scenario. "Roy, you old ballyhooer, you've come through for me at last like you said you would." Good heavens! She could almost love the guy. OK, so the lyrics pounding in her ears maybe did have something to do with it. 'It feels just like we never said goodbye,' sang Crystal Gayle.

The sky was blue, the road was wide and open, her credit card —courtesy of Colin, Annette had little money of her own—was in her purse. No man she could strictly call her own either. She had only to walk through the lobby of her co-op building to taste the gall of that. Once, at an open meeting of the decor sub-committee of the lobby committee, she had raised her hand. "Would the proposed wallpaper"—silver-flecked purple, a sample was passed round—"not make the place too gloomy, like a nightclub sort of."

Faces turned away, knowing eyes met, smiles tightened, the purple wallpaper went up. By what right did she voice an opinion? The pariah lady. In the whole building, in fifteen years, she hadn't made one honest to goodness friend. The women by and large scorned her; the men were amiable—when they were alone. Even the doormen—pleasant as they had to be because she tipped well—couldn't completely efface their thoughts. What was she supposed to do, wear an 'I Am Not Available' button. She'd actually slapped one of the elevator boys—in the days when such creatures existed—for making an obscene suggestion. Poor kid—from the talk down below he probably assumed she was aching for it. Well, maybe she was. It was no business of his. He was fired.

WELCOME TO PRINCE FREDERICK, a sign said. "It's hard to find a meat that's as versatile as Spam," drooled the radio DJ. New York City this wasn't. Not long now. Just a question of locating the Sheriff's office, presenting the lawyer's letter and obtaining a key.

"Nothing there," Baffle had said. "Place is a mess." It said so in one of his precious files. "Save yourself the trouble."

"I've nothing better to do."

A mess sounded promising. Roy usually left a mess, of one sort or another. She had to start somewhere.

CHAPTER THREE

The Calvert County Sheriff's Office betrayed no surprise when a red Caprice wheeled up to its door and a woman on the south side of middle age—eager and attractive in a comfortable sort of way—jumped out and presented a laissez-passer from a New York law firm. Almost as if they were expecting her. Yet Baffle hadn't mentioned alerting the authorities and could hardly have expected Annette to act with such dispatch. She put it down to sheer Southern equanimity. This was a different world all right from the one she'd just left. They even provided an escort, a good idea since she'd never have found the place on her own.

Once off the highway Annette stayed close to the gleaming white cop car as they zigzagged along minor roads plunged in the exuberant greenery of high summer. At length, at a ranch-style sign announcing in burned-in letters SCIENTISTS CLIFFS, they turned. Traces of human habitation began to appear—mown grass along the verges, ornamental trees, a clutch of empty tennis courts, scattered clapboard houses looking worn and lived in giving way to newer homes discreetly settled into their natural surroundings. Back of a field in which show jumps were set up sat a modest clubhouse with its attendant bevy of parked cars. A couple of miles and several forks in the road later her escort eased to a full stop in a leafy lane. As Annette lowered her window, a suffocating poultice pressed in on her. No wonder so few people were around.

The deputy sheriff—or whatever he was—slammed his car door and ambled over. "Well, this is it," he gestured at a low, brown-painted cabin among the trees. Great—for a hidey hole—

Annette thought. Other dwellings similarly withdrew snail-like into their shells. "Better pull in here off the road."

Annette parked the Caprice and got out. "What's the name from, Scientists Cliffs?"

"Bunch of scientific folk from Washington used to vacation here. That's where it came from to the best of my belief. All dead and gone. Guess the name stuck. It was a big ole farm and they bought it."

"And the cliffs?"

"Right down there's the Chesapeake." He pointed. "Full of fossils, the cliffs. They say at one time it was all under the ocean."

"Chesapeake Bay?"

"Yes ma'am."

Annette climbed the steps to the back porch, opened the screen door and tried the key. "OK to return it tomorrow?" She called out.

"Whenever you're through, ma'am, that'll be fine."

"Thanks, and thanks for showing me the way. Is there any place around here to stay?"

"On down the highway 'bout twenty miles there's a bunch of motels. Otherwise it's back to Frederick. Nothing too great there either."

He's put me down for the wife or widow, she thought, watching him reverse up the lane. Baffle, no doubt.

The porch door opened into the kitchen. It was a shade cooler inside, but the stench was unbearable. A quick look told her why. Garbage lay strewn across the floor as if a raccoon had ripped apart a bagful. Trails of black ants were carting stuff away. They had their work cut out. A cloud of flies rose desultorily and landed fast, apparently gorged. Annette passed quickly into the living room. Even Roy would have been hard put to leave behind the chaos there. Books and papers flung about, cushions piled up, ash and wood from the fireplace dumped on the rug, houseplants spilled from their pots. In the midst of it all, oblivious of their surroundings, a recliner and a television solemnly faced each other. Had he been sitting there, watching something, she wondered, and escaped in the nick of time? What tipped him off? How did he get away?

Annette's impulse, after moments of bemused horror, was to get away herself, get back in her car, and go. Silly woman. Big fat mistake. Then another sentiment took over: rage against whoever had done this. She picked her way to a door on the other side of the room. The bedroom. Drawers pulled out and tipped onto the floor, a mattress propped against one wall, pictures at odd angles. A walk-in closet—jammed with shirts, jackets, slacks, ties, shoes, coats and ancient suitcases—seemed to have escaped the havoc, as if whatever it was had run its course. Or perhaps they'd found what they were after. The room reeked mustily of old tennis balls. The bathroom, contrastingly, looked undisturbed, the medicine cabinet a museum of bygone remedies. Annette picked up a plastic container: *Valium. No more than eight tablets daily.* For a V. Botkyn.

She ran her hands under the tap, then tried the light, which came on. In the bedroom she fiddled with an air conditioner. Surprisingly, it rumbled to tepid life. Hands on hips she contemplated the bed until, in a fit of decisiveness, she grabbed hold of the mattress and grappled it into position. Once she had the bed made up and everything crammed back into drawers, she knew she would stay the night.

The bedroom window overlooked a leafy ravine that fell away abruptly behind the house. Leaning out Annette saw that another story was wedged into the angle formed by the slope so that on this side the place was double-storied and was bigger than she'd imagined. Back in the living room, she noticed a narrow staircase descending to a closed door, which turned out to be locked on her side. As she inched it open, frigid air seeped past her up the stairs.

Odd, she thought. Exploring further along an unlit passage she came to a door she pushed open. A black leather recliner dominated a small room. Beside it, sleek and black, towered a stack of complex-looking electronic equipment. On the seat of the recliner lay a pair of earphones, large ones, and stacked on shelves around the walls were records, tapes and CDs. An aloof orderliness permeated the room, in contrast to the mess upstairs. Roy had had a neighbor.

"Anybody home?" called Annette. A smell of pipe smoke suggested a man. "Anyone home?" A clock ticking somewhere, that was all. Locking the door behind her, she climbed back up the stairs, grateful at least for the quick chill, the boost she needed to tackle the living room.

So far she'd found nothing she could positively ascribe to Roy. The clothes could have been his, but her feeling was they were not. Apart from the fact that V. Botkyn—if it was his place Roy was renting—was a portly, Salvation Army was writ large. *Her* Roy was incapable of putting on weight—his low metabolism, he claimed, inherited from his dad. Plate after brimming plate she'd prepare, drawing on her Italian and Lebanese ancestry, plumping herself, never him, to blimp-like proportions till, in a panic, he'd insisted she take the rabbit test. He'd always been a bit of a

clothes horse. Hadn't Baffle described him as 'living in considerable splendor' as recently as a few months ago? With Roy, appearances mattered.

Methodically Annette set about righting the furniture. Here
too she found nothing that spoke to Roy, though many of the
books were conceivably his: Book of the Month Club and Literary
Guild selections, scarcely opened, unreadable, un-throw-out-
able. She stuffed *The Body Has A Head* back on a shelf. Roy de-
lighted in filling bookshelves by mail order though rarely— it
seemed to her in their four years of marriage—did he read further
than the blurbs. He saw himself reaching down a volume and
pressing it on some feebly protesting acquaintance with a few
well-rehearsed words.

What, Annette wondered, hefting a stack of Gourmet Mag-
azines into a cupboard, had Roy done in this room in the days or
weeks he'd lived here. Sat staring at the TV? And what, she wondered, shoveling ashes back into the hearth with a plastic table
mat, had his pursuers been after, besides him? The one thing she
could say for sure was this: Roy hadn't left this place in a hurry.
He'd had time to purge traces of his ever having been here. More
of a phased withdrawal than the desperate breakout of a cornered
man.

The kitchen Annette left to last. With a can of insect repellent
she advanced, paper towel clamped over her nose, on the rotting
trash pile, managing to enclose most of it in a green plastic bag.
This she dragged out to the porch and was standing in its shade
catching her breath, conscious of sweat trickling down her spine
and between her breasts, when a car pulled in and stopped with a
crunch of brakes. Pushing back her hair, she slipped into her
sandals.

The thud of a car door, footsteps on the gravel, and there he was. Sixtyish, square-jawed, grey hair slicked back, short-sleeved green sports shirt untucked over brown shorts, a slight limp, carrying two grocery bags. The downstairs neighbor. He passed so close to Annette that, by all the unwritten rules, he must surely acknowledge her.

No way. "Sir! Excuse me!"

He turned. "Tuesdays and Thursdays."

"I'm sorry?" Had she detected a European accent? Ah, it's about the garbage. He thinks I'm the new tenant. "Actually, I was wondering... Could I see you for a moment? It's—"

"Perhaps you will see me every day"—he set down his bags in a gesture of exasperation—"coming and going to my car. I cannot stop you. But to interfere with my privacy, that I will not permit. This is my last word. Good evening." With a curt little bow, he picked up his bags and hobbled down the path out of sight. Moments later she heard a door slam.

Annette leaned on the porch rail. Yes, it *was* evening. The sun slanting through the trees accentuated all the various shades of green. Somewhere up there a bird was mournfully singing, a whippoorwill perhaps. One phrase repeated over and over in almost infectious sadness, yet so loud. Had Roy stood here and listened? If so, what were his thoughts? The suggestion of a breeze touched her shoulders. She went inside, propping open the kitchen door. The place needed air. Then she took a lukewarm thought-provoking shower.

"Roylance Calvin Warrender,"—as the water splashed around her feet she noted that the varnish on her left big toe was chipped—"where the heck are you and what's going on in that hyperactive brain of yours this very minute?" He'd hated Roylance, and it took a while for Annette to extract it. He was persecuted in school and blamed his folks. His mother—her mind full of gothic fantasy—favored Lancelot. If Roy was good enough for him, his dad said, it was good enough for his son. They compromised.

Dinner was an apple Annette had brought with her and the peanuts from the plane. Cockroaches had gotten into the fridge, weevils into the rice and beans and pasta, ants into the sugar. Of the few cans, none appealed. She could have driven out to the highway but was afraid of getting lost. Besides, something told her to stick around, keep her eyes open and her wits about her. She wasn't here for the cuisine.

She made a mug of Sleepytime tea—what can happen to a teabag?—and collapsed into the recliner, feeling around for the remote. Aha, it had slipped down inside the arm. Except it wasn't the remote, it was *Spanish for Travelers*. The remote was down the other arm. Flicking channels, one came in clear, something about sea otters. How Roy had doted on those nature programs, and how often she'd dozed off in their cramped apartment to the mellifluous grunting of Bill Burrud's *Animal World*.

Flicking off the set, she opened the Spanish phrasebook and found herself looking at a photo wedged in among the pages. A small, grayish black and white of a thin-faced youth with an ambivalent smile and wing-nut ears. On the back, in her own twelve-year-old hand, was written, Roy in Mexico City.

So he *had* been here. She'd begun to doubt it. And why the phrasebook? Had he looked at the photo and thought of her? Imagine keeping it all these years, nearly thirty for crying out loud. Had he remembered the trip? It was their first encounter. Her father, a man obsessed with saving money, had come up with a textbook case of what he called 'affordable extravagance'. By combining a honeymoon with his second wife, a business trip, and an exotic holiday for the kids, he ensured that very little enjoyment would be had at one third the cost. In the book he'd never gotten around to writing: *How to Live Like a Millionaire Without Being One and Not End Up in Jail: The Shaheen Method*, the Mexico trip would have pride of place.

In a surprising gesture to Annette's fourteen-year-old brother, who'd taken the re-marriage badly, he invited the boy's best pal at school along for the ride. The surprise turned out to be Roy. The principal, deeming any member of the gang the lad hung with unworthy of such a treat, substituted a more deserving kid from a poor-white farm family. And Shaheen Jr. made it his business to make Roy's life far from pleasant from the get-go. It was Annette, alienated and confused at the onset of her first period, who found companionship in Roy. And gratitude.

As time passed, he didn't forget. He wrote, he visited. Seven years later they married. After the divorce, it occurred to Annette that there might have been an element of revenge in his attentions. Getting back at his tormentor, sort of. Perhaps it was the therapist put the thought in her mind. If so, Roy could have saved himself the trouble. Shaheen Jr. never made it as an adult. He breathed his last at a flophouse in Katmandu. Altitude sickness. That, at least, was the story.

CHAPTER FOUR

It may have been the Sleepytime tea, or more likely the heat and exertion of the day, that caused Annette to nod off. Waking, it was dark outside. She was slumped in the recliner. Her neck ached from the awkward loll of her head. As she massaged the spot and thought drowsily about turning on a light, a noise from the direction of the kitchen—a knock, a pause, then another knock—alerted her. She might have dismissed it only it came again, uncomfortably human in its insistence, yet not quite the rap of any human knuckle. Her neighbor downstairs, perhaps? There was something furtive and unwholesome about him, and much as she wanted to question him about Roy, she demurred. Her watch, in the darkness, glowed two-thirty. If she withdrew to the bedroom and locked herself in, perhaps he'd give up.

Leaning sideways, she'd an unobstructed view through the kitchen to the screen door. Light from a street lamp filtering through layers of leaves formed a perfect rectangle of cloudy orange, unmarred by human shape. Curious, and impatient with her imaginings, she approached and pushed it open. The porch was deserted. The stillness of the night rebuked her. Fastening the door on its hook, she was halfway to the bedroom when the noise came again, this time from the front door to the left of the fireplace, just a few feet away. As she looked, a shape stretched up, clawing at the wire mesh, pulling it open and letting it fall back.

Large and dark, it crouched behind the bottom panel staring up at her. A cat. "Poor baby," she cooed, easing the door open, "want to come in do you?" Next thing she knew, it was under the couch. "So, introduce yourself."

It occurred to Annette that *she* was the intruder, though nothing in the way of cat paraphernalia was in evidence. Had Roy been fond of cats? They'd never had pets, come to think of it. Oh, a gerbil, called George McGovern, but that was a baby-sitting chore. Could be this cat was just hungry. She turned on the kitchen light. Roaches sped in all directions.

To Annette, a hardened New Yorker, the sight of a cockroach had the effect a bugle call might have on a squadron of cavalry. Seizing the nearest weapon—a magazine—she laid about her. The next thing she knew the cat was at her side, pouncing on the critters, tossing them up and catching them, crunching them, swiping at them, scooping them out of tight places, rolling in them. A handsome beast with mottled black and yellow markings.

When, at last, she climbed into bed, the thing joined her, kneading the pillow and purring like a dynamo. She shoved it further down—bonding has its limits—though admitting, as she drifted off, that sleeping next to a warm and breathing body was something she wished she could do more often.

Despite her late night, Annette was up early thanks to her companion's interest in the birds singing alluringly just beyond reach. She carried a cup of tea outside and leaned against her car. The shadows were deep and long, the air not yet hot. Roy had chosen a perfect spot in which to disappear. The house—a pseudo log cabin construction—was so hemmed in by trees that a driver on the road only yards away might miss it. Some of the surrounding places had the anonymous midweek look of weekend retreats, the well-tended little lawns and shrubs of others spoke of retirees. An old man hanging out the flag, fumbling, taking his time, doubtless wondered who she was. Perhaps he'd wondered about Roy. The inevitable jogger loped towards breakfast with the morning paper, a spaniel at his heels.

Breakfast. A nice thought. Oh to get in the car and nose around in search of something edible, juice, coffee, a bagel, cream cheese. But no, weeks Roy spent here according to Baffle; she had but a day. The tally so far: a snapshot of a fifteen-year-old with sticking-out ears and all the memories that went with that, and a vision of his older self brushing up on Spanish in front of the telly. Was that all there was to show for it? She stared some more at the house, at the porch cluttered with broken plastic flowerpots, a rusty barbecue grill, firewood, the remains of an exercise bike. What had the cop said? *Right over there's the Chesapeake.* Setting her cup on the car's roof, Annette strolled in the direction he'd pointed.

The road sloped gently down past several plots before curving sharply to the right. At this point the houses on her left assumed a more substantial air. It was only when she stopped and looked out across a garden that she realized it wasn't all sky she'd been seeing. Somewhere in the haze, water and sky merged. A path plunging steeply through thick vegetation held the promise of the bay itself. She took it. Soon arching green boughs blotted out the sky and vines dangled like hawsers. As she picked her way down steps hacked from boulders and hewn logs, a rivulet bubbling and gushing by her feet, the feel became tropical. The more so when she saw at the bottom of the leafy tunnel a patch of white sand and stumbled blinking into sunlight.

The tide was out, the beach narrow, at points only a few yards wide. Steep wooden steps zigzagged from boathouses up the cliffs which stood fifty feet high—though slumped might better describe the slides of green-tufted shale crumbling onto the sand. As for the scientists, the cop was right, they weren't around. Nobody was. Annette shaded her eyes. Far away toward the horizon a tanker plied its trade, making for the open sea. Given a boat, Roy could have escaped this way, she supposed.

Damp and exhausted, Annette climbed back to the road. She'd have given a whole lot for a blueberry waffle with maple syrup and a long cold glass of orange juice.

"Good morning, out for a stroll?" She'd already noticed the elderly lady moving among her flowers, positioning herself for a chat.

"Just down the beach. Fabulous place you have here."

"Not from these parts, are you? I thought not. You're the new girl at Vladimir's."

The new girl at Vladimir's. A manicurist at the local beauty parlor, perhaps? "Afraid not." Annette smiled. "Who's Vladimir?"

"The Botkyn place," the woman pointed up the road. "You're not"—darting from behind a shrub and lowering her voice—"a relation of Randy Huff?"

On the verge of denying Randy, as she'd denied Vladimir, Annette remembered that Baffle had told her it was a name Roy was going by. Randy Huff. The tag just didn't fit. "In a way. Not strictly speaking, I suppose."

"I wouldn't ask," the woman said softly, "only I've something, well, a little awkward to suggest. I didn't think I could do it when all those men were here. Tell you what," she glanced at the house, "Hal's making breakfast. How about it?" She added, "He's a wiz with a waffle iron."

Talk about instant gratification.

Hal's waffles, while not blueberry, hit the spot. He'd already given Annette his secret pancake recipe and filled her in on his years at the Commerce Department in DC "before Reaganomics messed everything up." Margaret, the wife, explained about the cliffs and displayed a collection of million-year-old fossilized shark's teeth they'd picked up, while Annette worked her way gratefully through the waffles. She was on her third cup of coffee when Margaret made her move. "It's about Ozzy." She glanced furtively under the table.

"Ozzy?"

"One evening last month Randy knocked on the door and asked if we could take Ozzy. Said he'd be away for a few days and didn't want to leave Ozzy alone. Of course we agreed and that same evening Randy brought him over in his traveling basket along with a sack of Kitty Litter and a month's worth of cat food.

"Well, of course we'd no idea. I mean we'd seen him walking to and fro and said good morning and so on, but we really didn't know him at all. Just that he'd taken the Botkyn place for the summer."

"Seemed a pleasant enough fellow," put in Hal, "said he was in cybernetics."

"It's been much longer than we thought," Margaret hesitated, "and you know the rumors that can work themselves around a place like this, and then those men, and the police, and—but perhaps you have news, perhaps Randy'll be back after all. Do you think so?" She looked hopefully at Annette.

"I rather doubt it." She explained about her distant marriage and the Will.

"Oh, but that's wonderful!" Margaret clasped her hands in an unexpected gesture of relief. "You'll want to take him then, of course. Such an intelligent creature."

"If we're talking about a large black and yellow animal with a deafening purr"—it dawned on Annette they were discussing her inheritance—"he slept with me last night."

"So that's where he was. Oh Hal, isn't that wonderful?"

Just great, thought Annette. Especially as Colin can't be anywhere a cat has been within a year without having an asthmatic attack. Wonderful. "Are you sure you want to part with him? He'd be so much happier here than in the city."

"I know, but what with the grandchildren coming next week, and allergies and so on..." Margaret's voice trailed away.

"Way we heard it, guy owed a bunch of money and they lowered the boom," said Hal. "We don't expect him back. Mad as hornets they were when he slipped through their fingers. The Feds were here, the State Police, the Sheriff, you name it."

"How did he get away?"

"Got in his car and drove. Simple as that. Supposedly they had the place sealed off. Well, there's sealed off and sealed off, and then there's plain dumb." Hal tapped his temple. "Surprise ya?"

"There's talk he left by boat," Margaret put in. "There was activity down at the beach that night. The Halversons' dogs were going crazy. They had to lock them up."

"But in the morning, his car was gone," maintained Hal. "How d'you explain that?"

"The guy in the basement apartment at the Botkyn place, would he know anything?"

Margaret and Hal exchanged glances. "Old Schnitz? Talk about sealed off. Didn't know the cops were there, till they walked into the den. Or so he claims."

"What's the story there?"

Hal said, "You hear rumors. Taught shop at the local high school for years."

Margaret was less guarded. "My favorite is the one where he swam ashore from a U-boat in the war and is waiting to be activated."

Hal scowled. "There's a bunch of retired intelligence folk down here. You can't sneeze without a conspiracy theory."

Approaching the house, Annette's hopes rose. Old Schnitz was working on his car. Ranged around him were cleaning products of all sorts and shapes. At her tentative, "Excuse me?" he redoubled his efforts at a spot on the hood. Flecks of sweat sizzled on the hot metal so that she feared the veins on his neck would burst.

"Did you see much of the man who stayed here this summer?"

Abruptly the rubbing ceased. Grabbing a bottle of Fantastic, he turned on Annette, finger on the trigger. "Altogether too much. But not as much as I'm seeing his successor."

"Oh, you mean hardly at all?" She wouldn't be brow-beaten.

"He was not so impertinent to put his car in my space. Observe now the bird crap." Squirting in outrage, he applied himself again to the hood.

Heading north in the Caprice, Annette envisaged lawyer Baffle's face when she laid out for him the sum total of her inheritance: a cat. Oh, and a photo taken by herself twenty-seven years ago in Mexico City, not to mention a Spanish phrasebook . The face she tried *not* to envisage was Colin's when, on his next visit, his allergies started up; though, with luck, his ailing maharishi would keep him out of New York while she worked out what to do. Once he found out whose cat it was, she'd never hear the end of it. Colin and Roy had never met, but Colin had for Roy—based on hearsay—all the amused indifference a high roller on Wall Street might have for a creature in a betting parlor. Annette had never managed to convey to Colin any of Roy's even mildly good points. And he had quite a few, she reminded herself now, even if it took some winkling to get at them.

"Name one," Colin would challenge as he nibbled an earlobe, his idea of foreplay.

"That time he gave leftovers from our Christmas dinner to a beggar."

"And what did the beggar do?"

"That's not the point. The point is—"

"What did he do?" He was twisting her ear and it hurt. He remembered too well.

"OK, OK. Threw it into the trash."

Colin laughed maniacally. "Why?" He managed between spasms.

"Said he didn't care for dark meat. We'd eaten both breasts."

Annette smiled, thinking of the question she'd saved to the end to ask Hal and Margaret, to sound like a casual inquiry. With Ozzy duly delivered in his basket with a few cans of cat food and a small bag of Kitty Litter, Margaret explained that she'd stuck in some notes Randy made about his care and feeding. "Apparently he's particularly fond of Gorgonzola, though of course we don't eat full fat cheese and didn't have it in the house."

"Trust him to possess the only feline on earth partial to Gorgonzola." Annette shook her head. "How did he look, by the way? Twenty years can do a lot of damage."

"Trim and handsome, I'd say," Margaret laughed. "He'd a fine mustache too."

"Altogether very persuasive," Hal added on a less enthusiastic note.

"There was something," Margaret reflected. "His eyes. Sad. Like a pet goat the children had once."

Annette glanced over to the passenger seat, at the basket securely strapped in. Ozzy seemed restless, unable to settle down. She wondered what in heck she was going to do with him.

CHAPTER FIVE

"**P**erhaps now you'll be more inclined to take my word," smiled lawyer Baffle over his bow tie. Far below, through the plate glass window, Manhattan was suffering through another heat-crazed August day.

"And you mine," Annette shot back. She had described her visit to Maryland.

"On the contrary, I didn't doubt you for a moment. I know grit and determination when I see them. But tell me, now you're back, are you more convinced or perhaps less so that Warrender is alive?"

"Who said I was convinced at all?"

"Come come, Mrs Warrender, you are not that good an actress."

"Let me ask *you* something, Mr Baffle. What were they looking for, your people? It wasn't just a mess, Roy's place, it was pandemonium. Ashes dumped on the carpet, garbage all over the kitchen, drawers pulled out and everything strewn around. Disgusting."

Baffle conveyed the tips of his fingers to a point directly under his nose. "Not *my* people, Mrs Warrender. The forces of law and order."

"Disorder, more like."

"I assure you they were as perplexed as you seem to be. They didn't create that pandemonium—your word—they found it. The assumption was that Warrender left somewhat precipitously."

"Then what about his arrangements for the cat?"

"Puts an intriguing spin on it, I grant you. Tell me, Mrs Warrender, did your former husband have a soft spot for cats?"

"Not particularly, no, when I knew him."

"Is it a very valuable cat?"

She shrugged. "How did they trace him there, anyway?"

"A tip-off, I gather. Anonymous."

"And they let him just drive away?" Well done, Roy.

"The tip-off came too late."

"So how come you think he's dead?"

"I said, it's possible, that's all. They traced his rental to Dulles Airport. He was going by Randy Huff, as I mentioned. Someone of that name was booked on a flight out. A no show." Baffle rose. "Thank you for coming in, Mrs Warrender, you've been most helpful." He walked her to the door. "Oh, one other thing. I don't suppose you're in touch with his sister? Runs a little guest house down the Jersey Shore. Cape May, I believe."

"I'm afraid not." Interminable Thanksgivings with Al and Lenore had been one of the milestones of life with Roy.

"Nice, this time of year."

"Are you suggesting something?"

"I should have warned you about lawyers, Mrs Warrender. We're a mercenary bunch. We work for whoever pays us. We should walk around with cautions on us, like cigarettes. My business is to recoup my clients' money, as much as possible, as fast as possible. I'm not your lawyer, Mrs Warrender. I'm their lawyer." His parting words, as he closed the door behind her: "Feel free to be in touch."

Like hell, she thought.

The Ocean Guest House wasn't hard to find. Near the center of town on a corner lot, it was across the street from the boardwalk. Annette found a parking space some way off on a side street and was glad of the walk after two and a half hours of the Garden State Parkway. Cape May breathed a sea-side tackiness in refreshing contrast to the Manhattan where she lived and the New England where she grew up. Its pretensions were so outrageous that not taking them seriously amounted to being a spoil-sport in a make-believe children's game, and Annette found part of herself responding to the sheer vulgarity.

She climbed some weathered wooden steps, rang the bell and waited. A screened-in porch wrapped itself around the street sides of the building. The place had recently had a coat of paint. All was pink except for the shutters on the windows, which were mauve, and some chairs which were leprechaun green.

After a while Annette decided that she'd waited long enough. Early afternoon was probably a slow time hereabouts when people either swam or slept. The front door opened into a vestibule giving onto a passage. A door in the passage was ajar. "Anybody home?" She called out, before peeping in.

A body lay sprawled on a couch, partly covered by the sports pages of a newspaper. His mouth hung open and the flesh of his cheek—the hue of supermarket turkey—drooped against his shoulder. He might well have been dead, save for the slight rustling of the paper as it rose and fell over the belly of Annette's ex-sister-in-law's husband. He'd lost most of his hair in the twenty years since she'd set eyes on him. Overhead a fan turned listlessly.

Perfect, she thought. She'd racked her brains for a way to broach the subject of Roy. Circumstances had come to the rescue.

The staccato clap of her hands launched Al Dimly to his stockinged feet. Fighting off bits of newsprint, he groped around a desk and came up with a ledger and a pen. "Jeez," he half-glanced in Annette's direction, "must have dozed off. Was that just yourself now, or—?"

"Hello Al. I'm looking for Roy."

His double-take seemed genuine. "Oh my God!" He slapped his head with an open palm. "I don't believe this. I do not *believe* this. For crying out loud—Jesus, Annette!" They didn't move to embrace, or even touch. Soon after her marriage to Roy, Al Dimly had roused himself enough to make a pass at her. Not that she'd have objected to something with a bit of pizzazz. But his lackluster attempt to feel her up—as if she'd become some sort of shared serving wench—had disgusted her. Ever since, when they'd found themselves alone together, despite herself, she'd remember. And so doubtless would he, and for some perverse reason would encourage Lenore to suspect the worst. Which was probably why Lenore had kept her at arm's length.

"Just wait right here," Dimly backed away, "Lenore's upstairs. Resting. She's not going to believe this." He made as if to leave, then glanced at his watch. "Better give her a half hour. Needs her rest, that gal. I'm telling you."

Sedatives, thought Annette.

"Now what's this about Roy? You did say Roy, didn't you, or was I dreaming?" he laughed nervously. "You two back together, or what?"

"I haven't seen him in twenty years, Al."

"Wish I could say the same."

"See him often, do you?"

"With Roy, once a year seems often. So what gives? Behind on alimony payments?" Weak with mirth or perhaps a muscle spasm, he clutched the door for support. "Come on in the front room and take the load off your feet, assuming you got a minute." She followed him back down the hall. "Say," he declared, "you're looking great. So what's up? What's cookin' these days?"

The front room was furnished to suffocation with an array of chairs and couches. On the mantelpiece was a statuette in bright metal of a crouching figure. She picked it up. *National Marbles Tournament 1986, Wildwood, NJ. A. Dimly, 4th Runner-up,* was etched on the plinth. "Roy's gone missing. Seriously. I got a call from a lawyer. Apparently he owes a bunch of money and they're after him."

"He owes *me* money, and I don't care if I never see the SOB again. Listen, do me a favor and don't mention that to Lenore, that he's missing, OK?"

"How is Lenore?"

"Doin' real good. But this could push her right back down again. It's about Beth Ann. After Mitch and Rita passed they put her in a home. Which is not cheap, let me tell you, and Roy hasn't been coughing up his share. The old check's-in-the-mail thing. Apropos of which, a couple of months ago he calls with a big announcement. Everyone's worries are over. He has money coming in. Real money. So what else is new? First thing he's doing is getting a banker's check for Lenore covering Beth Ann for ever."

"June? Where was he?"

"Toronto, I assume. He didn't say. That's where he's been."

"So where was the money coming from?"

Dimly held up his hands. "Lenore took the call. If it'd been me answered, I wouldn't even have told her. Up and down, up and down, like he's got her on a yo-yo. Had her sold."

"And since then?"

"Zilch." He glanced at the time. "Listen, do me a favor. When she comes down, tell her she looks like a million bucks, know what I mean? She already lost eighty-five pounds at the fat farm. I'm telling you," his vacant eyes wandered the room, "it's not easy. We went way in the hole to get this place."

"It's nice," she had to say it.

Without warning, Dimly crashed his fist down on the arm of his chair. "Got it! They take off backwards, see." He flicked the fly away. "You gotta hit 'em where they came from. I'll tell her she's a pleasant surprise waiting for her downstairs."

When she saw who it was, Lenore tried not to look disappointed. Not Roy with the promised check. "Well, I declare," she declared, planting a big kiss on Annette's cheek and leaving a pink smudge. "Don't you look like a million dollars."

That's my line, thought Annette. "You too, Lenore. You're looking fabulous!"

"Oh, he tells everyone to say that," she turned on Dimly. "Haven't you offered our guest any refreshment?" He slunk from the room. "Sometimes I wonder why I didn't ditch that guy years ago." She didn't lower her voice. "Now it's too late, and look at me. You were smart and it shows. Get out while the going's good, eh? Al means well, but he's a loser. Same as Roy. Trouble with men, ninety-five percent of them are losers."

"It was Roy who ditched *me*, remember?"

Looking at Lenore, at the harshly lined face and staring eyes of an insomniac, she detected not the slightest glimmer of Roy.

Beth Ann, the sister she recalled from visits to the farm, was younger, prettier, not quite all there. She had Roy's long face and wide-set eyes. How fond he'd been of her. Then, mysteriously, she'd been hustled away out of sight. Annette, just married, remembered visiting her with Roy in the institution and having to leave when she became violent. Her baby was stillborn.

"The trouble with Roy, he doesn't know what's good for him. He goes with the wrong sort. I seen it again and again. Leaving you was the dumbest thing he ever did."

"Sometimes you only see the value of what you had years later, I guess." She felt ridiculously weepy.

"Look at me," Lenore appealed. "I hung on." She lit a cigarette and blew out the smoke.

"I'd like to see him though," Annette confided. "You know, older. Who knows? Al mentioned that he called you."

Lenore leaned back to peer in the direction Al had gone, then dropped her voice to a low rasp. "You're not the only one. A man was here a few weeks back, asking questions. Mark my words, something's up. I didn't tell Al on account of his blood pressure'd go over the top."

"A lawyer?" Baffle, she thought, the weasel.

"Some kind of investigator. Flashed a badge. I told him to get lost. It's that strumpet he married that's all the trouble. You ever meet her? Led him a royal ride in the fast lane, let me tell you."

"How long did it last?"

"Twelve years. Her father was a big Mucky Muck up there. Toronto. You'd think they were royalty, the way they carried on. In twelve years you know how many times we got invited. Count 'em: three. They didn't want to know us. Left him for a horse trainer in Texas."

"Arizona," corrected Dimly, backing in with a trolley. "Diet grape or iced tea?"

"Cut him off without a dime."

"So he claimed."

"Took the kid, too."

"Kid?" Annette wasn't sure she'd heard right. Odd Baffle hadn't mentioned it.

"Another disaster," Lenore said. "She spoiled him rotten. And he went along with it, Roy did. I'm not letting him off the hook. Half the time they'd no idea where he was. A little savage. Remember that dinner, Al? We're sitting with the silver candlesticks and goblets and all and this troop of ragamuffins marches in. Shane—that's the kid—grabs a bunch of linguine off his mother's plate, stuffs it in his mouth, says 'Yuck' and they go on through to the kitchen. A few minutes later, they march out munching stuff and drinking what looked to us like beer. And Al says, What's the drinking age up here? Because none of them looked more than twelve. Don't worry, Roy says, We keep the hard stuff locked up."

"How old is Shane?" Annette asked.

"Fifteen, sixteen?" She looked at Al. "If he hasn't burned himself out. Try one of Al's muffins."

"Cranberry-orange, coffee marshmallow..." Dimly recited, poking them. She picked one he hadn't touched.

"The one thing I'll never forgive him for," Lenore said, "is raiding Beth Ann's fund."

"They were joint signatories," Dimly explained, "and he forged Lenore's."

"He must have been desperate, that's all I can think. He loved her more than I did."

"How did he sound when he called?"

"Excited. It's finally coming together, that's what he said. And not to worry if we didn't hear from him for a while. He planned to set up a new fund for Beth Ann. Toronto hadn't been good to him, that's what he said."

"Any idea where he was off to?"

"Wouldn't say. But he mentioned Shane, how he wanted to be a proper dad to him, which he hadn't been. Funny thing," she exclaimed, "last weekend I brought out your old wedding album to cheer myself up, and now here you are. Perhaps I'm psychic."

"I don't suppose Roy ever spoke about me, did he?"

"No, he never did..." She left it hanging. "Al, go up and get that album, the red one on the dresser."

When he returned, they buried their heads in it. "Some nerve we had, just look at the length of those skirts."

Annette's heart went out to the awkward young bride who had so much yet to learn about life. It wasn't a plush affair. Her dad hadn't thought enough of Roy for them to merit that. Most likely he didn't expect it to last, and didn't live to know how right he was. Her stepmother diplomatically did not attend, leaving the field to Annette's aunt from California who managed, with her enormous purse and determined chin, to hog center stage.

The man to Roy's left, towering over his diminutive parents, was Kjelborg, his best man, whose first name Annette could never remember, if she ever knew it. Roy just called him Kjelborg. "Roy worshipped him." Lenore said when Annette pointed him out. "Used to bring him to the farm and poor Beth Ann fell for him head over heels."

Before leaving, Annette managed to obtain an address in Arizona for Shane's mother, saying she'd be out that way and would be curious to look the boy up.

Shane, Annette decided driving back to the city that evening up the Garden State, held the key to Roy's whereabouts.

CHAPTER SIX

In the matter of Ozzy the cat, it was Mrs Wing who came to the rescue. Or perhaps it was her small grandson, Mark, who sometimes accompanied her to Annette's and sat reading in a corner. Ozzy's nerves were taught as strung piano wire. He had taken great exception to the flight from DC, and Manhattan—with its cacophonous aural fireworks making normal street conversation impossible—tortured the eardrums of a sensitive cat. Annette had never visited Toronto, Ozzy's presumed hometown, but knew it had to be a whole lot quieter. Released from his basket, he made for the furthest, darkest corner of the apartment and stayed there for two days. Here, under the bed in the guest room, Mark found him. Ozzy and Mark became playmates and, in the course of an uninterrupted morning, grew attached.

A day or two later, Ozzy and Mrs Wing shared a cab out to Yonkers, where Ozzy began a new life as a paying guest on the ground floor of a two family house on a leafy block. Annette copied out Roy's instructions on his care and feeding in block capitals—Roy's writing being cramped and small—leaving out the bit about Gorgonzola. She was filing the original in her recipe draw for lack of a better place, when printing on the verso caught her eye: P A E A N, it read in soft brown brushstrokes, with some green fir trees dotted artistically among the letters along with birds on the wing. Underneath, a line of small print read, *Protect America's Environment: Act Now.* And under that, in even smaller print, *Kjelborg & McKenzie*, a box number in Ottawa, Canada and a phone number. It appeared to be the top half of a sheet of otherwise blank office stationery.

Before she had time to think through what she was going to say, Annette was dialing the number. It was just too much of a coincidence. After a few rings, a recorded voice told her to dial the first four letters of the party she wanted to reach. K J E L invoked an instruction to recheck the spelling and dial again. P R O T received another reprimand. P A E A, however produced more ringing, and a third disembodied voice told her that her call would be answered in the order in which it was received, and that she was to have herself an environmentally conscious day.

Annette waited, anxiety mounting as to how to explain herself to Kjelborg, who surely had forgotten her existence and was having an environmentally conscious afternoon in some cool office in Ottawa. So that when her turn came, annoyance was tempered with relief at yet another recording. This one started with some bars from the Ode to Joy, and a voice-over (Kjelborg?)—saying—chanting almost—"Paean, a hymn of triumph to Apollo, a multitude of voices raised to Protect America's Environment! Act Now! Leave your message at the beep."

Startled, she blurted, "It's Annette Warrender. You probably won't remember me. It's about Roy," and left her number.

Plans for Arizona were revving up. With Ozzy taken care of, there was nothing really to keep her in New York. The more Annette planned and schemed and worried about Roy, the further receded the so-recently almighty Colin. She'd considered contacting London to make sure he wasn't back from India and heading her way, but in the end didn't. Deep down—while not quite liking to admit it—she relished the idea of his walking into an empty apartment. Let him do the waiting and wondering for a change.

Annette was of two minds as to how to approach Roy's other ex. Tucson, Arizona, was a long way to go to drop in on someone unannounced. And Selina Warrender had become, somewhat dauntingly, Mrs G. Randall Frampton, so she couldn't pretend she'd spotted the name in the phone book. Finally she decided to play it straight and bank on the other displaying, at the very least, curiosity.

Either Selina Frampton was bored, or she was still browned off enough at Roy to want to lap up any sort of dirt about him, or —perish the thought, it was only mid-morning in Arizona—she was a little tipsy. But whatever she was, she seemed intrigued by the call and could hardly contain her amusement. "It's like Roy's the flavor of the month."

"How so?"

"You're the second call I've had about him recently. What's he done now?"

"Nothing, that I know of. Well no, that's not quite true. He's disappeared. Seems like he has creditors after him."

"So that's what it's all about."

"What?"

"Someone snooping around, asking crazy questions."

"A lawyer?"

"Police. They said police. At any rate, who cares? Roy can go to hell as far as I'm concerned." Her advice to Annette was: pack a bikini, take the next plane out of New York, and stay as long as she liked. There was plenty of room. They would, she promised, tear Roy to shreds around the pool and scatter him to the desert breezes.

When they met at the airport, Annette surprised herself by instinctively liking Selina. On the phone, she'd sounded a bit far-fetched—perhaps the anglicized Canadian accent—but she'd a directness about her gaze, a chin-upness, that Annette responded to face to face. As they sailed across town in a snazzy roadster, Annette saw in this stranger an image she aspired to: the silver-streaked hair tied back casually in a ponytail, the fresh-cheeked vitality, her confident way behind the wheel. A wave of self-doubt swept through her. Compared with this, she was bargain basement. Why would Roy bother with the likes of her when he'd had a dozen years of this near-perfection? Only later did aspects of Selina appear which cheered her up.

It was the pool—set at 90 degrees—around which Selina's life revolved. The setting was idyllic. On the one hand the comfortably sprawling ranch-stye house nestled amid trees and flowers sustained by sprinklers going almost non-stop; on the other, the sweep of the desert—the place was on the very edge of town—culminating in the purple ridge of the Catalina Mountains, which rose like a velvety backdrop at the edge of the world.

"I used to speculate about you," Selena volunteered as they lounged side by side on deck chairs, drinks in hand, staring up through the cactus-filled canyon towards a jutting finger-like peak—the finger of God some called it, Selina said. "You were Roy's dark secret. It was years before I discovered he'd been married. No photos, no mentions, apparently no memories. Everyone's entitled to one mistake he said, when I found out. You're not what I visualized."

"Do I disappoint?"

"Quite the reverse. One fine day in the office, the story went, he came to terms with the fact that he was twenty-two and unmarried. Scrunching up a memo he was drafting and lobbing it into the trash, he pledged himself to the next single female who spoke to him. Down the aisle came trip-tripping the new temp, a short-sighted dimwit with braces and bad breath. Our hero balks, makes an end run for the men's room, and almost knocks down a perfect stranger. Profuse apologies. 'Don't mention it,' says you. The die is cast."

Annette laughed. "Deceitful bastard. I'd known him since I was twelve."

"It was years before I realized he was a pathological liar."

"He's off somewhere now, reinventing himself, I'm convinced."

"In due course a Better Roy will burst on the scene to sweep another useful innocent into his dubious embraces." Selina drained her drink. "I should have cut out years before I did. Or better still, not got hitched at all. You were wise to duck out quickly."

"It was Roy did the ducking out. As far as I was concerned everything was fine. One day I came home early from my Christmas job in the handbag department at Saks, to find Roy in his overcoat with his bags packed. He seemed cold and distant, like a ghost. He slipped the note he was writing into his pocket and said, Look, I can't talk now. The cab's waiting. I asked where he was going. Canada, he said. There's a terrific job opened up. I said, What about me? Or something equally pathetic. I felt like slapping him. I'll call you, he said. And that was the last I saw of Roy."

"Fucking coward." Selina spat out. "Roy all over."

"If Dad hadn't left me a small trust fund, I'd have been up the creek. He'd cleaned out the bank account. Would have taken the trust money too, only Dad—being Dad—sewed it up tight. Must have had the whole thing planned for weeks. Some Christmas, that was. If it hadn't been for therapy, forget it. Later, I gave him his precious divorce right off, and he very thoughtfully sent me an invitation to your wedding."

"Oh my God! Tick *tack*." Selina fixed herself another drink at the mobile bar.

A young Mexican—Annette had seen him gardening around the house—approached, dangling a large lizard-like creature. Smiling mischievously, he held it out to Selina. "Oh, Pedro, take it away, take it *away*," she cried, spilling some of her drink.

"Gila monster," he addressed Annette.

"Poisonous, horrible things, they hide under the house. I told you not to kill them." They watched him walking away, his broad, bare torso gleaming in the late afternoon sun. "That's one thing Roy didn't have much of. Sex appeal. Or maybe he did, or why did I marry him? What do you think?"

"It wasn't obvious," Annette was thoughtful. "It grew on you. The excitement of a salesman making a pitch, kind of. Not that we didn't take it seriously. We studied *The Tao of Love and Sex* together and all that."

Selina shrieked. "Yuck, the Seventies! I mean he was fun at first. He swept me off my feet with his courting. I'd never seen anything like it. I mean the jocks I hung out with, their one and only concept was to fuck. Roy came on in the grand manner. Champagne and roses, ski slopes, fancy restaurants. Money flowed. He'd serenade me outside my window on his harmonica, stuff like that. The guy had flair. Of course it was the Pepsi Canada account he was really courting for his agency, and maybe they were footing the bill. At the time, it never crossed my mind.

"When couple swapping was the scene in Toronto—I mean what do you do there in winter?—Roy disapproved, scared of us catching something, he said. Well, he was right. I caught Randall, a real live honest-to-God hunk of man flesh. Any more of Roy's promises and pious prevarication and I wouldn't answer for the consequences."

Randall, Randy Huff, thought Annette.

"The thing I finally figured out about him was, it all boils down to money. If he's got it, he's OK. No matter if it's his own, the bank's, or someone else's. Without it, his inferiority complex takes over and pulls him down like seaweed and he's dead in the water. Twice Pops bailed him out. When he finally cut him off, that's when Roy had his breakdown. He'd cry for days at a time at the prospect of bankruptcy court. He'd disappear, come back, disappear again. He was pulling me down with him. He threatened to kill us both. Get this: in front of Shane, he threatened to kill me. I swear he meant it. Pops and Randall drove over that night and took us away." Selina's voice grew hoarse with the memory. She gulped her drink.

"It didn't take Roy long to turn defeat into victory. At first he wouldn't even talk about a divorce. Then he changed his tune. He virtually sold me and Shane to Randall for big bucks."

"He let the boy go without a fight?"

"Are you kidding! He was scared of Shane. He'd created this child monster and was, well, flummoxed. Hadn't a clue. After the divorce he bought him a cat. Can you imagine? Knowing perfectly well I was allergic. I sent it right back. Randall has his own kids. He didn't want Shane either. He only agreed because of me. In the end it didn't work. We had to put him in a special school."

"Nearby?" Annette asked hopefully.

"Colorado. We tried a local place but he kept escaping. One time we came home and found him with a friend terrorizing the cook with a pair of dueling pistols from Randall's collection. They were both loaded—the boys not the guns thank God."

"I'd like to look Shane up," Annette said, with less enthusiasm than she'd originally had for the idea.

Selina jumped at the suggestion. "I'm very bad about going there," she confessed. "Haven't come to terms with what he represents I guess. Never wanted kids anyway, beastly little buggers. Unlike Roy who's heart was set on them, at least in theory."

At forty-three, Annette wondered, could I still have Roy's child? Talk about a wild idea. Selina was staring at her with alarm writ large across her face. "Good grief, woman, you're still in love with the bastard!"

CHAPTER SEVEN

G. Randall (GeeGee) Frampton didn't appear for dinner. No explanation was offered and Annette didn't like to ask. For all she knew they were separated, though this seemed unlikely given the amount of GeeGeeana cluttering the available surfaces, many extravagantly dedicated. GG darling, from Zsa Zsa, type of thing. Selina's penchant for man flesh was fully born out in the photos: though more Ralph Kramden than Tarzan.

"Randall's originally Albanian," she volunteered while the soup course was being cleared away. "Oh, meet Gloria. Keeps things going while I laze around the pool, don't you Gloria?" Gloria smiled a distant Mexican smile.

"Randall has a place in Toronto. You could stay there if you're headed that way. I'd suggest my folks as well, only with the Roy connection it might be too weird. Mention Roy and Pops goes ballistic." Toronto hadn't occurred to Annette. It seemed the last place Roy would be.

As excited as she was about the quest, Selina needed a grand finale, something suitably cathartic to lay Roy for ever to rest. If he'd died or come to harm, she wanted all the grisly details. She needed him hounded and caught. "Whatever happens," she speared a shrimp, "the one person you've got to get hold of is Kjelborg."

Kjelborg, again. "Are you in touch?"

"Not any more. But if anyone can lay hands on Roy, he can. They were very close. He knew all Roy's secrets."

Annette told her about the call she'd made to him in Ottawa. "He'd crash at the apartment every so often; on the floor because our couch wasn't long enough. Fine with me, he was Roy's best friend. Super laid-back. I remember ironing a shirt for him once and burning a hole in the cuff. He laughed it off. It irritated Roy no end."

"Yeah, Roy had his prudish side."

"I can't imagine him having an affair."

"You know, I really don't think he did. Odd, particularly when he started his own PR business. I mean, what is PR? Stewing for hours in expense account restaurants with overheated dames. *L'amour* grows like mold, I'd have thought. No, it was only after I walked out that the fun began. Hog-wild with teenagers, flaunting it all over town."

"Teenagers?"

"Practically." Selina poured more wine. "Of course it was all aimed at me, but it backfired. I mean, for all its size, Toronto is a small town. It can only swallow so much before throwing up. He became a laughing stock. I actually felt sorry for him. He'd turned forty, and that's hard enough for anyone, and he let it all just run through his fingers."

Annette glanced reflexively at her own fingers while Gloria cleared dishes. Life running out. She knew all about that, and suspected Selina did too. Coffee was served in the sunken living room where a wall of glass gave onto the canyon and the starlit sky, as if they'd landed on some uninhabited planet. The only sounds, the slurp slurp of the leaf-gobbler in the pool.

"Between ourselves, if you ever do find Kjelborg, be alone with him in a closed space at your peril. *Droit de seigneur* and all that." Annette wondered, but Selina didn't elaborate. "At first, I couldn't figure out the relationship. Here's Roy, a workaholic checking the time every three minutes, serious about clothes and wine and working out and the movie of the month, and here's this large, soft, out of shape, cynically bemused pseudo-small-college-English professor type in a crumpled suit and suede shoes, with a gleam in his eye, who at any moment might break out in an outlandish dance step like in the middle of some boring cocktail party. It was a while before I twigged: Kjelborg is what Roy would like to be but knows he never will be because he's too tight-assed insecure. Kjelborg is Roy's court jester."

They talked on into the night, working through a bottle of Remy Martin. Annette found herself speaking of her life with—and without—Colin with a frankness that not even her coffee kvetch group was privy to. In turn, Selina poured out the story behind the story of the elusive Randall who, she said, only really wanted a brood mare for his ghastly kids; and threw in details of a torrid affair she was having with a driving test instructor at the Arizona Department of Motor Vehicles.

When, eventually, they supported each other to their respective rooms, Selina, breathing heavily, laid a restraining hand on Annette's arm. "Don't do it," she pleaded.

"What?"

"Throw yourself away for that bastard."

As she collapsed into sleep, Annette, who'd taken 'bastard' to mean Colin, realized it was Roy Selina was warning her about. "How dare she?" she thought, languidly struggling to get up. By morning, she'd forgotten all about it.

Selina drove Annette to the airport where she hopped a plane north to Flagstaff and rented a car. Skirting the Grand Canyon with its bittersweet memories of a long ago trip with Colin, she headed north-east for Four Corners. The driving and the feeling of sheer space did her good. Desolate, open country, the occasional herd of cattle, a few horses. Traffic was sparse: the odd car or pickup, then a half hour with the road to herself. She crossed the vast plateau of the Navajo Reservation with the sun dropping down, isolating weirdly weathered stands of rock in its fiery glow. A feeling grew that she was dodging the shades of an old life, and if she could make it through these sentinel-like rocks, she'd be safe. Four hours, five hours, it was dark before she finally found a motel that showed signs of life.

Next morning, feeling curiously unburdened, she crossed the Colorado state line and, following Selina's directions, turned north at Durango. Purgatory, the sign said. The road climbed for several miles following the flow of a river. Mountains loomed all around, grayish blue in the distance, heavily wooded in shades of green from silvery to dark, closer at hand. The sagebrush-covered plains fell away behind her. Before Purgatory she turned off where a board said, discreetly, BUCKHAVEN. Once a hunting and fishing lodge, now a prison, Selina said. They—whoever they were—expected a Mrs Warrender, though Annette wasn't entirely clear what her relationship with Shane of that ilk was supposed to be. "Don't let them bully you," Selina had added, ominously.

All the same, the watchtowers caught her off guard. At one moment there were aspens shimmering silver round a small lake. Then, poking above them, the towers—two that Annette could see. Forest fire beacons, she wondered, straining to see if they were manned. Rounding a bend, she came abruptly to a roadblock and scrunched to a halt. A man in uniform came out of a hut. After some words on a walkie-talkie, he strolled over and raised the barrier with his foot.

A mile or so further on Annette slowed for a series of speed bumps and saw the fence. It twisted away up the valley, a ribbon of mown grass on either side with every so often a tower. So this is where the rich bury their problem offspring, she thought, pulling up to another checkpoint. The guard flipped an expectant two fingers at her. Handing over her driving license, she eyed a gun stuck in its holster at his hip. Do you shoot to kill or just maim? she wanted to ask.

Apparently her credentials checked out. She was waved through and directed to a long, low cabin-like structure where cars were parked around a flagpole. "Be sure and remove your ignition key and lock all doors," the guard cautioned, "and the trunk."

The principal was a florid gentleman with a military haircut, suspenders and a short-sleeved open neck sports shirt straining to contain a beefy torso. Not till the interview was over did Annette realize he was in a wheelchair. As they talked he checked and rechecked a clipboard, stealing disconcerting glances from it to her, almost as if trying to catch her out. "We at Buckhaven are the upholders of a proud tradition. In our thirteen years here, the Buck hasn't suffered a single loss, not one we haven't caught within twenty-four hours. We proudly stand behind our pledge to refund fees for the entire year in such an eventuality." Was he quoting verbatim from the prospectus? A sign on the desk said: IT STOPS AT THE BUCK.

Brandishing a 7 iron, he jabbed at an ordnance survey map on the wall behind him. "Within our boundaries we maintain a semblance of normalcy. Boys wear their own clothes, grow their hair any way they want, carry on as they would in an all-male secondary level institution on the outside. We call this, Tactical

Defusion. The more militaristic approach that many of our brother institutions resort to makes an explosion inevitable, we feel. They exit like a cork on a bottle of warm champagne, straight into the jailhouse. We want our graduates to say, Hey, we worked things out at the Buck, we can work things out in the world!"

Trotting across the yard in the wake of the principal's motorized chair, Annette felt that maybe she'd misjudged the place. A woman came towards them, the bracelets on her arms jingling and glinting. "I'll pass you on to Miss Pattison, our inter-community relations director." This accomplished, the principal veered away.

Miss Pattison also knew the trick with the clipboard. She looked at Annette, then back at it, then back at Annette. "Mrs Warrender?" Annette smiled and nodded. Miss Pattison looked relieved. "This is what we call our Kiva Room, where meaningful staff-student interface takes place, usually on a one to one basis." Opening the door with a key, she announced in a sing-song voice, "Shane, your grandmother is here."

A thin, pale youth sprawled, legs apart, in one of the two chairs in the small room, his paleness accentuated by his all-black get-up. Long, stringy brown hair partially eclipsed his face and the crudely executed tattoo of a skull on his bare upper arm. His wrists were as choc-a-bloc with bracelets as Miss Pattison's. Around his neck hung a silver cross and the front of his T-shirt spelled, in electrified lettering, MEGADEATH. Expensive-looking cowboy boots, draped in chains, adorned his feet. He stared at Annette with reluctant curiosity. Before he could speak, she put a finger to her lips.

"I'll let you two go to it," Miss Pattison announced cheerfully. She hadn't seen the signal. "You'll have so much to talk about. Back in half an hour." They heard the key turn in the lock and listened to the diminishing jingle.

"You gonna like spring me outa here?" Shane growled. He had Roy's appealing grey eyes and high cheek bones, and an indolent fullness about the mouth which was more his mother's. Noticing him casually in other circumstances, he might have passed for a girl.

Annette took the second chair. Grandmother, indeed. Thanks a lot, Selina. Shane eyed her critically, his thoughts perhaps running on similar lines. "You might at least have worn like a wig or something."

"You sound as though you were expecting me."

"Not like now, man. Roy said the fall."

"I know," Annette lied. "I'm casing the joint."

"I got it all figured out, OK?" He leaned forward, keeping his voice low. "Gimme the trunk key. Then while you're back in the office—like drag it out a bit, OK—I got a friend who's gonna cause a diversion during which I get into the trunk." He rippled his fingers. "The key plus a hundred up front for the kid. What have you got for wheels?"

"It's not going to work, Shane. If Roy said the fall, Roy means the fall. Between you and me, he's out of the country. What else did he say?"

Begrudging every movement, Shane extracted from a pouch around his waist a minutely folded paper. Smoothing it, he held it up out of Annette's reach. "What's a four letter word for a furry fairy in claws instead of boots?" he challenged.

"Why, Ozzy," replied Annette without skipping a beat.

CHAPTER EIGHT

"Cool," Shane was impressed and couldn't help showing it. "You into Sabbath?"

"I'm thinking more Ozzy the Cat."

Shane's face lit up. He let go the paper he was holding. It seesawed down until Annette caught it. She'd already recognized Roy's handwriting.

Darling Son, she read, *Hang in there. Your old Dad loves you—whether you know it or not, whether it always seems that way or not. Don't ever for a moment forget that. Right now— you'll no doubt be amazed to hear—he's getting his act together and taking it on the road. Goodbye Toronto. Believe me, the only thing I'll miss about this burg is that little rubber puck, and without a certain enthusiast beside me on the bench, the charm has worn thin there too. Hang in, as they say, till fall, and I'll check with you again. Till then, over and (get it) out. Roy.*

At the bottom, he'd written: *Ozzy's coming with me, so be cool. After all, he's the nearest thing I've got to a certain crazy 15 year old metalhead.*

Shane shifted uneasily in his chair. When Annette finished reading, he said, "Got a light?" and held out a cigarette. A sign on the wall said, NO SMOKING. Slowly she folded the letter, then leaned over and tucked it into a rip in the knee of his jeans.

"Sorry, kicked the habit. Listen Shane, Ozzy's safe with me. Till Roy gets back or till you do, whichever comes first."

"I love that cat." She could tell he was pleased by the way he wiggled his foot. Perhaps it was the only love he could admit to.

"That's some kickass fuckin' cat." After a moment's silence, he said, "You like, his fuckin' girlfriend?"

She smiled, "I'm just an old gal from New York City, someone your Dad knew way back before you were born."

Shane brightened, "You mean, like, a call girl?" The idea seemed to appeal to him. He sat up. "Shit."

"Roy and I go back a while. We've had good times together."

"Roy smoked a dude once. I'm not supposed to know, but I know."

"What do you mean? Be serious."

The jingle was coming back. "So where do you crash in New York?"

She told him. "Ask for Annette."

"Annette. I'd like that." He said slyly, "Like maybe I'm into older women."

The key turned in the lock. Some weird kid, she thought, taking care not to smile.

Later, at the exit, a guard sauntered around the car and gestured for her to open the trunk. For a panicky instant Annette thought they'd find Shane curled up and gazing at them with that strange, sad, disquieting smile.

Annette caught a flight home from Denver early the following morning. As soon as she entered the apartment, late in the afternoon, she knew something was up. For one thing a bunch of fresh mail from the box in the lobby was sitting on the foyer table.

"Colin?" She called, inquiringly. "Colin?" The place was empty, but it hadn't been. A bed in the guest room had been slept in. And next to it—oh mute reproach—was a trashcan half full of tissues. She looked for a note, any sort of communication. Nothing.

The answering machine registered seven calls. The first, a wrong number, the second and third trying to sell something, the fourth, Colin. He was at the hospital—presumably St. Barnabas Uptown, where he taught—with the maharishi. Surgery was imminent. No time or date. He was absolutely all in. (Colin? the maharishi?) and looking forward to a light dinner and an early night. The fifth and sixth calls were hang-ups. The seventh message—Annette balked at listening—would be Colin again, excoriating her for whatever.

But the seventh call, it turned out, was not from Colin. The seventh call was a voice she hadn't heard in twenty years. Beginning with a low, rich, fruity rumble, it segued into a warm, rib-crushing verbal hug. "Annette, Annette, little stranger, voice crying in the telephonic wilderness, what took you so long? I've waited lo these many moons and well nigh abandoned hope. At a day's notice I will wing my way to your side, scoop you up in my unencumbered arms and plant on your chaste brow the imprint of my unworthy lips. Seriously, always there's business to be done in the Big Apfel. So brave once more the new world of touch-tone tomphonery and tell me your pleasure at the beep. Ciao ciao." Kjelborg didn't give his name. He didn't need to.

So taken aback was Annette by this bravura performance that she let the tape run on for about a minute wondering if Colin could have heard it. The nerve! Even back then she'd hardly known the man, and yet, *He knows all Roy's secrets.* OK, she'd call, but not just yet. Her first call must be Selina, to report on her visit with Shane and, not incidentally, his boast about Roy smoking someone. Say it isn't so, was all she needed to know.

"Bloody damn!" She heard before even announcing herself.

"Are you alright? Hi, it's Annette."

"Smashed a perfectly good G&T. Otherwise, fine. What's up?"

"Went like clockwork with Shane. I think we bonded, to some degree. One thing though: he rather casually threw out that Roy *smoked* someone—in Toronto I guess—and that he wasn't supposed to know but he knew."

"Oh my God, how did he know? He couldn't have been more than five."

Annette's heart stopped. "You means it's true?" She was relieved to hear laughter at the other end.

"Can you imagine Roy actually killing someone? A person. I mean with his bare hands, this was supposed to be." Annette had to admit that she couldn't, not her Roy. He was more likely to have been the victim. "Exactly," said Selina. "There was absolutely no evidence."

"But there was a *murder*?"

"Oh God yes. Daughter of good friends of ours. Society people. Gem of a girl. They never caught him."

"Him?"

"The killer. The boyfriend had a cast iron alibi, they said. Which always makes one suspicious. Nasty piece of goods."

"Where did Roy come in?"

"It was lunchtime, rather a seedy part of town where she was trying to make it on her own, slumming basically. Roy was visiting one of his artists nearby—who did work for the agency. The police asked anyone in the area at the time to come forward, so the silly bugger does and they call him in for questioning. Pretty soon he's so obsessed by the whole business he thinks perhaps he did it. He was actually going to confess. He totally lost it. I was ready to commit him."

"But he didn't?"

"He would have—but for Kjelborg."

Kjelborg yet again. "What happened?"

"Ask him. He'll tell you how he single-handedly saved Roy Warrender from the Chair which, by the way, is illegal in Canada. Though facts never bothered Kjelborg very much."

Standing at her bedroom window by the new drapes, which Colin, likely as not, hadn't noticed, Annette engaged in a little internal skirmish. Whether to call his London flat—it was too late for the office— or book herself a round trip ticket to Toronto and forget about Colin for the time being.

She'd been drawn to the window by a staccato flurry of birdsong so penetrating and varied that it might have been canned. Now the concert began anew. Perched on a high balcony—the bedroom overlooked the backyards of buildings on the side street—the songster, a lone mockingbird, yodeled his heart out for a mate. Wasn't that Roy: a mockingbird, singing all those different songs, none really his own? Who was Roy, really? That fifteen-year-old in Mexico City with the thin face, wing-nut ears and ambivalent smile. Yes, yes, yes. That was Roy.

Annette walked over to the phone and began to dial.

FAX ONE

Sent to: SURGE, LONDON

Sender: IN VESTIGIUM, INC., NEW YORK

August 26th

With reference to your stipulation that our office keep you posted on developments at least on a weekly basis rather than waiting for pay dirt, the following is as near as we can come for now to a reconstruction of the previous two weeks in the life of the Observee, hereinafter called the Obs.

To date our investigations have centered perforce on credit card data and calls made from your apartment in New York. In the future we anticipate more thorough reportage based on personal observation, electronic surveillance and other tried and true methods, bearing in mind your caveat that at no point must the Obs be even the slightest bit suspicious, and that, in the event, we call off the operation pending your instructions.

On Friday August 14th, the Obs flew from New York to Dulles International. There she rented a car which she returned the following day with 173 miles on it, suggesting a journey within a radius of seventy or eighty miles of the airport. We have no record of where she spent the night. For the return trip, Dulles to New York, she paid for two adjacent seats on the plane. In view of your caveat, it seemed unwise at this point to question the doorman on duty that afternoon as to whether the Obs returned alone to her building and, if not, to obtain a description of a companion.

On Monday, August 17th, the Obs rented a car in New York City. That same day she stopped for gas at a rest stop on the Garden State Parkway, the rest stop before the Atlantic City exit. She returned the car that evening with 330 miles on it. The rental agency records indicate no registered driver besides the Obs.

Three long distance calls were made in the time period. One to your London office and two, on consecutive days, from the New York apartment: a three minute call to Ottawa, Canada, and a five minute call to Tucson, AZ. The Ottawa number we traced to a voicemail service with a roster of clients where calls are routed automatically. There is no way of telling to whom a particular call goes. However, in view of the exhortation in the message on the Obs's machine (which you played back for us)—'brave once more the new world of touch-tone tomphonery'—it's a good guess that this was the Ottawa call on the rebound so to speak. We have provisionally designated this party, Ottawa Man. The Tucson number—officially unlisted—we traced to a business, Randall Estates & Enterprises. We are running a check on this.

On August 22nd, the Obs flew from New York to Tucson, AZ. There's no record of where she spent that night but, the following day, she flew from Tucson to Flagstaff, AZ, in the northern part of the state. Two days later, she flew back to New York from Denver, CO, having rented a car in Flagstaff and left it off at the Denver airport. Again, no record of where she spent the night. The area boasts several scenic attractions, including of course, the Grand Canyon, and we are checking out the principal hotels both in her name and the Randall name, though no Randall was flight-listed on the Tuscon-Flagstaff leg. The Obs gassed up in Durango, CO.

On August 25th, the Obs placed a second call to the Randall number in Tucson, duration 10 minutes, followed by a call to a travel agent. The following day, the Obs flew to Toronto. We will continue to keep you informed through this office.

CHAPTER NINE

The first thing Annette did when the bellboy, pocketing a hefty tip, closed the door on her suite in Toronto's downtown Royal York Hotel, was return Kjelborg's call. This time the recording skipped the Ode to Joy and all the rest of the nonsense and went straight to the beep. Annette was ready. "I'll be in the Library Bar of the Imperial Room at the Royal York tomorrow night at seven," she said, adding unrehearsed, "Well, you said a day's notice."

Irrationally, she felt a surge of warmth towards this man and was afraid, when she hung up, that it showed. With Selina's veiled warning in mind, she was leery of stoking a fire implicit in his message. On the whole, men who were attracted to her and made no secret of it—and there'd been a few—were usually the least appealing. The diffident were always to her more interesting. The trouble was, well, their diffidence. Which was one reason she'd been faithful to Colin—bar a couple of minor flings—for so long.

The Imperial Room's Library Bar was as lugubrious as its name. With the hands of the clock approaching seven, already several make-out artists had her in their sights. Repressed Canadian business types in tight detachable collars and conservative suits, likely bracing themselves in clutches of cozy masculinity before calling wives in Winnipeg or Medicine Hat and heading out on the town. An attractive woman drinking alone—needing fortification she'd ordered the advertised King Size Birthbath martini, a mistake in retrospect—seemed somehow more vulnerable here than in New York. Only one of them hadn't so much as glanced in her direction: graying, owl-like, beyond diffident to indifferent, he dictated into a machine in a briefcase that lay on the seat beside him.

With a day in hand before her rendezvous—assuming Kjelborg showed—Annette checked the phone book for Roy's number. It was still listed. *The number you have reached has been disconnected,* a voice announced frostily. She'd noted the address, and after breakfast took a cab out for a look-see. Babylon-on-Yonge billed itself as the latest word in downtown condo living. True to its name, garlands of greenery draped from balconies, roses and pelargoniums garnished every nook and cranny, fountains tinkled. She wondered how it fared in winter. In the recessed driveway, a doorman in white topee and golden epaulettes settled some grandee into the back of a Bentley.

Squinting into the brightness, Annette fumbled in her purse for her shades. What she saw appalled her. For the first time since she sat with lawyer Baffle she found herself doubting Roy and herself were on the same planet. Not that he'd died—she couldn't bring herself to believe that—but he'd moved into an orbit she not only was intimidated by but didn't aspire to. How could he possibly afford this?

Well, he couldn't. This thought cheered her up a bit. Why then, why had he done it? To spite Selina? To prove himself in the eyes of their fast-track friends? To impress clients and business contacts? Lost in disappointment and speculation, Annette was startled when topee and epaulettes loomed up beside her. "Pardon me, ma'am, but would you mind moving this way a step or two?" A line of cars was signaling to pull in. How long they'd been beeping at her she'd no idea.

By 7:30 Kjelborg had still not shown, and with every sip of the diet coke she'd ordered as a chaser, Annette's hopes ebbed. A new cast of characters thronged the bar. The owlish man with the briefcase had been joined by a woman who seemed more secretary than date. Then, as the minute hand on the grandfather clock began its climb to the top of the hour, she noticed one or two heads turn towards the lobby entrance. Conversations began to sputter and fade, and soon all eyes were fixed on the door.

A disheveled giant of a man stood in the doorway. For a moment he glared into the dim interior, a supporting hand on each jamb. Samson in the temple of the Philistines. Spying Annette, he advanced, repeating his mantra, she will, she won't, until, kneeling on the plaid carpet at her feet, he ended with a fervent, "She will!"

"Will what?" asked Annette, immediately regretting it.

"Marry me, I mean, forgive me—for being *en retard.*"

"Forgiven," she said, ignoring the first suggestion which, in any case, she wasn't sure she'd heard correctly. People continued to stare, if obliquely, or try not to.

"A mere twenty years."

"Kjelborg," Annette urged under her breath, "get up."

"You're making a spectacle of yourself," he mimicked. "Not until you kiss me." He protruded his lips, and to get the thing over with she bobbed forward and smacked him a quick one head on. With a few creaks and groans, camel-like, Kjelborg got to his feet. "Sic transit and all that rot," he puffed.

He was indeed greying and fatter, she noted, with crinkles around his eyes. At least he had most of his hair, which once—in both color and unruliness—had reminded her of straw. By and large the years, if not kind, had been tolerant to him. "For God's sake, sit down." Annette pushed a bar stool out with her foot, aware that eddies of distaste swirled around them.

Perhaps Kjelborg felt them too. He glared about the room like an actor who pretends to discover for the first time that he has an audience. "Annette, my pretty one, let me take you away from all this."

"What was that about?" She asked, in the lobby.

"I forbid you to inhabit these dark, satanic halls a moment longer. The moon shines bright. In such a night as this lets us stroll the wild sea banks deep in philosophical contemplation, if only of the seafood we choose to embed our molars in. Or, *in which* we choose to embed out molars."

"All right, I surrender," she begged.

"So soon? And the night so young?" He hailed a passing taxi which whisked them away she knew not where.

He was right. The Harbourfront was a pleasant enough place as night came on and a breeze off the lake dispersed the heat of the day. There were crowds and noise and, in between, pockets of shadow and quiet where the screech of a gull late to its roost was the only jarring sound. The subject of Roy was, at first, scrupulously shunned, though Annette felt it hung like a weight between them.

Kjelborg, indeed, proved himself a master of the art of talking and saying nothing, hiding—when she tried to pin him down—behind some facetious quotation or other. "Haunts of coot and hern," he rambled, when she asked where he'd come from. As for what he was doing, he was "involved in various enterprises of a lucrative nature, nature being among the least lucrative."

"All that stuff on the phone, the Ode to Joy and so on, was that you?"

"Joy? I know no joy."

"Well who was so exuberantly declaiming about saving the planet? If not Kjelborg, perhaps McKenzie?" *Kjelborg & McKenzie.* She recalled the logo.

From the sideways glance he gave her, she knew she'd scored. They walked a few steps in silence. "So, have you heard from Our Roy at all?"

"No. Well, in a way."

"Aha?"

"If you must know, I found your number on a bit of stationery on the back of which Roy had jotted instructions about cat food, specifically gorgonzola."

Kjelborg stopped abruptly. They were in front of a hotel where a debutante's ball—by the look of things—was getting under way. Limos disgorged shrill young couples in evening dress, others milled around. A young man bumped unceremoniously into him. He hardly seemed to notice. "Gorgonzola!" he cried. "I'm suddenly ravenous. Come on, let's find something to eat."

CHAPTER TEN

Kjelborg chose a fancy Japanese place jutting out over the water. Once they'd ordered and the waiter had poured wine, he raised his glass. "To auld lang syne!" They clinked. "Go on. I'm all ears. So you're back in touch? A spot of cat-sitting, I gather."

"Not exactly. It's been twenty years since we had any contact." She quickly filled him in on the call from the lawyer, Roy's mysterious disappearance, and her irrational urge to find him: Cape May, Scientists Cliffs, Tucson, Buckhaven and now Toronto. The chance perhaps for the two of them, older if not wiser, to start again where they left off. Kjelborg listened raptly through the sushi.

"So it popped into your head to give your old pal a call. I blush at the honor."

"Well, it was really Selina who gave me the push. And since I had the number on that letterhead, I thought, Why not? Maybe it's a sign. I wasn't at all sure you'd remember me."

"That lynx. I wouldn't put much stock in anything she says. Why me, one wonders?"

"She said, You have to talk to Kjelborg. He knows all Roy's secrets."

"Does he indeed? The bitch."

"I surprised myself in kind of liking her. She claimed that you, single-handedly, saved Roy from the electric chair. What was that about?"

Kjelborg groaned. He looked pleadingly at Annette as the waiter cleared dishes, bowed, and left. "Look here, old thing, do we really want to wallow in this particular mud hole? I warn you, it's exceedingly boring. I'd much rather hear about your lost twenty years. You certainly appear to have thrived."

"Please go on," she urged, "I'm in the mood to wallow."

Kjelborg grimaced, stretched, disentangled himself from a fishing net draped quaintly above their table, swallowed some wine and looked out over the water. "Once upon a time," he began, "in an exclusive arrondissement in the fabled city of Toronto, there dwelt a handsome middle-aged going on young ménage à deux called Kim and Tad Haggard. Their offspring, Jason and Jonquil, twins, lived with them. Kim Haggard had a daughter by her first marriage, called Kristi Aranda. Her father, a Spanish diplomat—if I recall correctly—had died.

"Kim Haggard was one of those dynamic, saintly women who move and have their being at the heart of society's most luminous circles, yet appear to remain unspoiled. A heart, in many ways, is what she was, pumping the blood around, keeping it fresh and clean. And she was rich. On the boards of all the worthiest and most fashionable charities. Born to wealth and privilege, she yet had all the down-to-earth qualities anyone could ask for in a friend.

"It was through her charities that she met Roy. He was shrewd enough to convince his bosses that, by donating their services here and there, good things would accrue. All Roy had to do was stage a couple of fund-raising extravaganzas which were wildly successful and he was—like the proverbial Flynn—in. Roy became the go-to man, the Wunderkind with the Midas touch. He set up on his own and business flowed his way. And the Warrenders and the Haggards became personally intimate. I don't know that the Haggards spent any time at all at the Warrenders, but the Warrenders were over at the Haggards whenever they felt like it. From the couple of times I tagged along, the arrangement seemed lopsided, but Roy and Selina didn't see that at all, and Kim and Tad were tolerant. Frankly, I found the set-up a bit disturbing."

"In what way?"

"My toadying allergy kicked in, I suppose. Imagine, it's Christmas Eve around the fire chez Haggard. I might mention that their place was like a wing of the Escorial, all halberds and marble. Roy is fondling one of the twins on his lap, Selina—a martini or three over the eight—is shrieking at some risqué joke of Tad's. And there's a bloody great cue-card—for the benefit of yours truly: see how palsy-walsy we are with the nearest thing to royalty Toronto has to offer."

A waiter was hovering, but Annette—with a suspect in her sights (who told risqué jokes no less)—paid him scant attention. "Tell me about Tad."

Kjelborg allowed a bib to be tied around his neck. He looked like the jaded toddler in a messy baby ad. "Tad, as in Thaddeus -one-of-the-Twelve, was third generation rich. Old money, for Canada. His passion was yachts, sailing the damn things around the world, palling with the likes of the Aga Khan. Worshipped Kim and the twins by all accounts, but from afar, more like another guest, when I was there. A cameo appearance, you might say, as the doting father. Younger than Kim."

"Much younger?"

"Oh, five years. More Roy's and my age."

"What about Kristi? Did she get on with her stepfather?"

"Crewed for him that summer. Taking a year off before college."

"She died, what, in the fall?"

"Late fall, it must have been. Poppy Day. We'd had our first snow. Veterans' Day to you."

"You were living here then?"

"Here and there."

"Tell me more about Kristi."

Kjelborg sucked out a couple of lobster legs and waved them around. Butter dripped from his chin. "Straight A's, swim team, sunny disposition, out to save the world."

"She'd moved out of the family home, right?"

"We *are* well briefed. The lady Selina, one supposes."

Annette smiled. "As little time as she seems to have for Roy these days, this is one thing she's not trying to pin on him."

"Guilt by association was her particular nightmare, I recall. Because she thought it *was* Roy, I'm convinced. And where would that have left her? As far as the Haggards and their crowd were concerned, in the same boat as the wife of the Yorkshire Ripper. You're too innocent, my dear, to comprehend this, but she did her best to get Roy to check into the local loony bin. Anything to get him out of the way. When that failed, she used all her feminine wiles to get me to persuade him."

"Warning: I may not be as innocent as you imagine," she said. Then quickly, before he could trot out some sugared adage, "Getting back to Kristi—"

"As Selina may have told you, she rented a couple of rooms above a laundromat, somewhat iffy neighborhood way out west on Queen; got a job in a nearby art gallery. On her lunch break she'd go back to her place and crash for an hour, so legend had it. On the day in question, when she didn't return to work, nobody went to check. That evening the boyfriend found her, sprawled across her bed."

"Tell me about him."

"They met that summer in Europe, sailing. Moroccan, I think. Apparently Kim and Tad had no idea he was in town, or even that they were dating. And they thought Kristi told them everything. The police were so sure they'd got their man they held onto him for days. Turns out he had a cast-iron alibi."

"Those are the ones to watch, Selina said. She thinks it *was* him."

"He'd flown in from Paris that evening. It all checked out. According to the medics, she'd been dead for hours. It was eight o'clock when they found her.

"Roy and Selina practically moved in with the Haggards—at least with Kim—because Tad was sailing off the Dry Tortugas or somewhere and couldn't be raised. By all accounts, Kim was a model of stoic motherhood. Selina, I shouldn't wonder, blubbered enough for all of them put together. And Roy, God help him, went around self-flagellating because he'd been in the neighborhood and thought of looking in to see if Kristi could use a bite of lunch. And ended up at Police HQ swearing out a statement to a detective sergeant from Homicide."

"So that's what happened." Annette had barely touched her food. "And you're sure about the stepfather. No way it wasn't him?"

"He simply wasn't around. But the fun was only just beginning," Kjelborg waved an admonitory claw. "When the boyfriend theory collapsed, they needed a substitute, and fast. This ain't New York. Murders are *causes célèbres,* particularly juicy society ones. They don't just fade away. Re-enter Roy in sacrificial lamb's clothing.

"His story checked out: he'd been with one of his artists, left him a bit after noon, and was back at his desk by Two. Said he walked, picking up a bite en route. So much for opportunity. What about motive? It didn't take them long to come up with one: Roy and Kristi were having an affair, Roy finds out about the boyfriend, there's a fight and he strangles her."

Annette choked and reddened. Pretending she had something in her throat, she took a swig of water.

"Only it was all circumstantial. No evidence of an affair, no one who could fix Roy at the scene of the crime. And when Kim herself insisted on putting up bail, they caved in and let him go. And that was that. There was a theory about a prowler—one of those face-saving fabrications—and the police went with that. If you're really interested, go check the files at Police Headquarters."

"But what did Selina mean about you saving Roy from the Chair?"

Kjelborg laughed sourly. "Did you ever come across Roy's paranoid identical twin? Calvin, I used to call him. Well, he put in an appearance around that time, moved in you might say. Calvin pointed out how quick they all were to turn on Roy—the outsider, the son of the dirt-poor Connecticut tobacco farmer, and so on and so forth till he had Roy fairly frothing with impotent rage. And finally Calvin turns round and says, Hey, so tell them, as long as they're so convinced already. Tell them Yes. Tell them what was going on right under their turned up snouts. Rub their noses in it. All I did was shoo Calvin off. A one-way ticket on a trans-Canada express."

"I guess Roy felt a bit that way towards my people," Annette mused. "It kills me to think of him now, a hunted man. Maybe

Calvin's reappeared. If I could only find him, I'd sit him down and say, Look, it's only money. It's not the end of the world. We can sort it out. Did you see much of him before he took off?"

"He did his best to avoid me, not that I'm here much these days." Kjelborg tipped back his chair, dislodging a glass buoy that crashed to the floor behind him. He didn't look round. "I lent him money, quite a lot in fact. Nothing kills a friendship like borrowed money, take it from me."

"Was that to do with your Save the Planet thing, Kjelborg and McKenzie?" She watched a busboy sweeping up the glass.

"Oh that? Yeah, well that was a while ago. Odd, that he kept that scrap of letterhead. I mean lucky he did or we might not be sitting here tonight. I don't suppose you have it on you?"

She reached for her purse, then remembered. "It's at home. I just have the number."

"You know, Annette, it was in the stars for us to meet again." He gazed out to where they should have been. She saw his hand creeping across the white tablecloth like a giant, hairy slug. For a while it fussed with the carnation centerpiece, then lay inert, inviting. She let it be, thinking of Selina.

"Did you know any of Roy's girlfriends? Selina mentioned there were quite a few."

"Had a bit of a scrimmage with one at a party, did Selina. Regular scratch-up. Made the papers. It was after that she was banished to the desert. Then there was a starlet in one of the soaps, *Society's Child*. Or was it, *The Evil that Men Do?*"

"What about when he disappeared, was he seeing anyone?"

"As I say, we were on the outs. But yes, from what I heard there was someone. A graduate student. Religious studies, that last infirmity of noble minds."

"Here?"

"PIMS. I forget what it stands for. Part of the U of T."

"You wouldn't know her name?"

"I wouldn't. But if you hang around the campus and question the lovelorn you'll eventually net her." He added quizzically, "You're very dedicated to this, aren't you? Why?"

"I told you: the road not taken, and all that."

When the waiter brought the bill Kjelborg pounced on it. Annette watched, amused, as he patted one pocket, then another and another, then stood up and began all over again. She recalled Roy's tales of the lengths Kjelborg would go to avoid picking up a check. "What the devil?" He muttered, peering under the table.

"Let me, please." She produced the requisite credit card.

"But I had it. I paid the cab."

"I paid the cab."

"I mean from the airport. I definitely had it then."

As it turned out, the bartender back at the Royal York had it. "Lady turned it in," he said.

Kjelborg checked and found nothing missing. Nevertheless, he seemed put out. "Can you describe this female?"

"She was with the older gentleman who was sitting over there." He pointed to where Annette had seen the man with the briefcase dictating.

"When was this?"

The man looked at the clock. "Maybe an hour ago."

Out in the lobby Kjelborg glanced about uneasily. "Did you get the impression at all that we were being followed?"

"Followed?" Annette was surprised. "Whatever for?"

Kjelborg shrugged. "Maybe it's just Calvin."

FAX TWO

Send to: SURGE, LONDON
Sender: IN VESTIGIUM, INC., NEW YORK

August 28th

Our check on Randall Estates & Enterprises reveals the following. A Toronto-based holding company, it is controlled by one G. Randall Frampton, 65. A Canadian citizen of Albanian extraction, with homes in Toronto, Palm Springs and Lexington, KY, as well as Tucson, AZ. He is known principally as a racehorse breeder, but his interests range from real estate to frozen chickens. He appears to be an immensely wealthy man with a wide network of powerful friends and enemies. He is married with three adult children.

On her arrival in Toronto, the Obs checked into the Royal York Hotel. Next morning she went by cab to the luxury condominium development where Frampton has an apartment. She stood outside on the street for some minutes staring at the building and, at one point, had to be moved along by a doorman as she was blocking the driveway. She made no attempt to enter the building, and returned to her hotel.

At 6:45 PM the Obs entered a street level lounge in the hotel and ordered a vodka martini with a twist. Towards 8 PM, an individual entered the lounge fitting our projected characterization of Ottawa Man. He proceeded directly to the bar and, falling to his knees beside the Obs, said, "Marry me." They kissed though beyond that the Obs did not encourage his advances. Indeed, they appeared more like old friends than lovers.

The pair then proceeded by cab to the Harbourfront area of Toronto, where they walked deep in conversation. At this time a watcher was able to 'borrow' the wallet of Ottawa Man. As this 'loan' was underway, he was heard to exclaim, "Gorgonzola!" His name is Soren Gustavus Kjelborg, a 47-year-old white male with a Post Box address in Edina, Minnesota. We will run a check on him and follow up leads presented by the contents of the wallet, should it be pertinent. The Obs and Ottawa Man ate dinner at a Japanese restaurant on the waterfront, engaging in animated conversation. She paid. They parted at her hotel. Watchers followed Ottawa Man to a nightclub where he sat for two hours over a few beers before proceeding to a nearby YMCA, where he was staying.

CHAPTER ELEVEN

The tram barreled self-importantly down the middle of Queen Street West. It passed a sizable park and, further on, some warehouses, and Kjelborg said, "We're getting close, I think." Annette took in the quaint parade of buildings, mostly no higher than three stories, hardly two alike. Here and there the scene was brightened by a startling paint job or the neon sign of some fancy little boutique. "Ten years ago," Kjelborg said, "this was a Mecca for artists, low-rise, cheap, a tram ride from downtown. The tide of Yuppie trendiness grazed its shore, eventually 'retreating to the breath of the night-wind'. Maybe the artists are safe for a while longer."

An old lady in the seat in front of them gathered herself up muttering, and moved across the aisle. Annette had noticed the beer on Kjelborg's breath too. He needs a strong woman to keep him in shape, she thought. What would her friends back in New York make of it: here she was, traveling with her ex-husband's best man to the site of the unsolved murder of a teenage society girl, of which murder her ex had, at one time, been suspected. Aren't we over obsessing just a bit? queried a voice inside her head.

Kjelborg reached up and rang the bell. They stood in the road while he scanned the block. "Shucks, did we pass it? Or did the laundromat close down?"

Annette likewise looked around, the tram already obscure in the shadows under a bridge. "You were here before?"

"With Roy, during the rite of self-exorcism he insisted on. A glutton for punishment, if ever I saw one. In Sybarites' clothing.

Oh the deep doodoo he got himself into, if you'll pardon the expression." And I had to get him out of, he implied. They entered a store that proclaimed itself a tattoo parlour. A discreet sign said, Acupuncture. "Was this a laundromat at one time?" demanded Kjelborg of a diminutive Chinese woman behind the counter.

"Laundromat?" She looked around, bewildered. "No, no, no, no."

Kjelborg stepped into the road for a better view of the building: brick, three storied. "I'm sure that's the door. See the number. And those were her windows," he pointed to two at the top in stained glass. "Wait here a second." He approached an old man a little way off in a doorway. "Yes, it's the place all right. The laundry closed. He even remembers the murder, and for a dollar could name the killer."

"Be serious." Annette eyed the man.

"Go on, ask him." Kjelborg thrust a dollar coin at her. She waved it away. "Afraid of the truth?"

Through the glass panel of the inside door, a narrow flight of steps, grungy and worn, disappeared into darkness. Up those steps had gone the feet of a man; down them those of a murderer. She tried to envisage the shoes, working her way up the legs, the waist, the shoulders. "Kjelborg," she said, over loudly in the confined space, "Yes or no, did he do it?"

"Would you settle for an honest answer?"

"Yes."

"I don't know."

Out on the hot street, Kjelborg turned to her. "Would it make any difference? Would you go on wanting to find him?" He seemed different this morning, not the blustering man about town, the swashbuckler of the evening. "Suppose he doesn't want to be found?"

"I won't know till I find him, will I?"

Kjelborg put his face in his hands and dragged them down over his chin. "Vouchsafe unto us patience, O Lord," he invoked, and Annette recollected that they'd been seminarians together, he and Roy. "What do I have to do to convince you he's not worth it? Prove he's a serial killer? Or would you then have to try to reform him?"

Annette ignored the thrust. "Do you know where the mother and stepfather live?"

"No."

"I thought you said you'd been there?"

"Years ago. They could be anywhere."

"Where they lived *then*."

"'Hello, I'm Annette Warrender. I think you knew my husband.'"

"I'd like at least to go by the house. Just to see it,"

As they moved off, a thin voice called after them. "Fifty cents, take it or leave it, Mister."

Hunching forward in the back seat of a cab, Kjelborg gave directions. They were in a very different world from the one they'd left just fifteen minutes ago, a self-assured world of substantial homes and quiet, tree-lined streets. 'Now take a left. Pull over there, behind that red van." He pointed across the road.

Annette took in a castellated mansion in rust-brown stone, partly covered with Virginia creeper. It stood four square to the road, its porte cochère advancing onto a ridiculously narrow strip of lawn. A stand of blue spruce contributed a whiff of the wild. The blinds on the leaded downstairs windows were, for the most part, down. The place had about it a sealed air. "It looks uninhabited."

"Most of the palazzi around here are at this time of year. Why stew in the rank humidity of a Toronto summer when the Riviera beckons, or Key West or The Cape, or a Lindblad tour of the Yangtze Gorges?"

Gazing at the stolid pile of stone, with the light catching the diamond-shaped panes, Annette had the sense that tiny signals were being transmitted, as if someone was trapped and needed help. She thought of the girl who'd died, cut off for ever at eighteen. "Was Kristi born here?"

"Probably not," said Kjelborg. He seemed anxious. A white, red and blue police cruiser had crept up and was dawdling at a discreet distance. "We better move. They'll think we're casing the joint."

She turned for a last look at the house. From a downstairs casement, a ghostly face peered out, its nose a pale smudge against the pane. A spaniel?

Kjelborg had a flight to catch, so Annette asked to be dropped off at PIMS at the university, which the cabbie had never heard of. Again, Kjelborg navigated. "Believe me," he told her, "I'm as concerned for Roy's welfare as you are. Perhaps a little more objectively, that's all. So let's keep in touch." She looked unconvinced. "Hey," he yelled, as the cab pulled away, "I'm a fan!" And he blew her a kiss.

In Annette's experience, people who said 'Believe me' weren't trustworthy, and people who blew kisses were full of hot air. On both counts, she hoped Kjelborg would prove an exception.

The Pontifical Institute of Medieval Studies, despite the grand ring of its name, inhabited a rather cozy, albeit crenelated, corner of the far-flung University campus. The wood-paneled room into which she wandered had a pleasant, scholarly feel with tall windows and a minstrel gallery, and an array of comfy looking chairs, in one of which a man was asleep. Annette eyed a busy noticeboard and a bank of pigeon-holes and considered her next step. She'd passed up an elderly priest who'd smiled at her, but when a young couple burst in and flopped down damp with heat, on a sofa, she took the plunge.

"Excuse me," she moved towards them, "I wonder if you can help me?"

They eyed her expectantly, as if there was nothing they'd rather do. After an awkward pause, the man said, "Sure. How?"

"Well, I'm looking for someone."

"Who?"

"A student." They waited. "That's it." Suddenly it was their problem. "A young woman."

Panic lighted simultaneously in the couple's eyes. "Do you know her name?" The woman spoke, enunciating each word.

"No," Annette smiled.

"A lot of students are away," the man said. "Vacation."

"She was in love. I think."

"With—your son?" The woman trod delicately.

"Exactly," Annette lied. She was beginning to see her way.

"And?"

"He treated her shamefully."

"You don't know her name, but you want to put things right?" The woman was into it.

"Precisely," she said gratefully.

"Here's what you do," put in a sleepy voice behind them. "You put a sign on the board. You put your son's name. You put a phone number and the message: 'To Whom It May Concern. Urgent Please Call.' And the date."

A dirty feeling, like guilt, clouded Annette's thoughts as she sat in the Vietnamese restaurant on College Street waiting for Roy's medievalist lover. The girl—woman—had sounded so eager on the phone, so pathetically concerned for Roy and his welfare. Annette had found a message already waiting on getting back to the hotel, a number to call 'after six'. Then on the phone, without divulging their relationship, Annette had to explain that she'd had word of Roy, but no, he wasn't back yet. On the board at PIMS she'd confined herself to WARRENDER, misleading but not quite the outright deception the sleeper at the Institute had advised. The girlfriend, whose name she hadn't caught—Bonnie or Ronnie—when pressed to name a rendezvous, had hemmed and hawed then suggested the Vietnamese place, near where she lived. "Ordinarily you'd be welcome here," she said, "but there's some kind of party tonight and it might be noisy." Annette could hear sounds like an orchestra tuning up.

The restaurant was narrow and small and almost empty. Annette sat at a middle table facing the street. She was early. People walked by the window like waves on a radar screen, each one trailing their special aura. A hard-faced woman out for cigarettes. A young black guy. Two more women, talking. She observed them through a jungle of plants—real, fake and painted on the glass. A string of lights alternated green and orange, on and off. Piped-in croony love songs in a tongue she wasn't aware of—Chinese, Vietnamese?—had folks at a back table singing along, anticipating the words. It made her sad. A waitress brought her tea. On the street the trams slid back and forth.

Annette stood up. A woman who'd walked by a few minutes before—rather too slowly for who she seemed to be—was standing across the street, as if waiting. She didn't look like Annette's idea of the medievalist—too old and put-upon—but you never knew. Had she meant to meet *outside* the restaurant? Annette stood in the doorway and waved, glimpsing the woman in between spurts of traffic, unable to catch her eye. A tram stopped at the light. It moved, and the woman was gone.

Precisely at eight, a small figure clad in what might have been a brown burlap sack with holes cut in it, slipped through the door and into the seat across from Annette. "Hi," she said, in a pleasantly husky tone, "I'm Bronwyn." Shooting an anxious glance across the table, she picked up the menu as if for cover.

"Oh, it's *Bronwyn*, is it? How quaint. I wasn't sure." Annette, determined not to patronize this innocent plaything of her ex-husband, found herself doing just that.

"Who are *you*?" Bronwyn asked, not unreasonably, flashing another shy glance. She was pale and slight with dark red wiry hair, almost black, pulled severely back and tied with a rubber band.

Overcompensating for the tone of her opener, Annette said, "Actually, I'm Roy's first wife."

The effect of this on Bronwyn was electric. Her face radiated such reverence that Annette had a flash feeling of what it must be like to be Our Lady of Lourdes, or the Madonna of Guadeloupe. "He told me about you. He said it was the dumbest thing he ever did in his life."

"Marrying me?"

Bronwyn blushed. "*Leaving you*. He said he'd go on paying for it till the end of his days."

"Roy said that?" Annette had to dab her eyes. Suddenly everything was wonderful. The lights blinked merrily, the crooning was just for her, the laughter at the back table echoed her mood, and a dusty, ribbon-decked plant in the corner—relic from a bygone Grand Opening—seemed to hold itself a little more proudly, as if to say, 'Folks, don't give up on us cast-offs just yet.'

CHAPTER TWELVE

May 25th is the day on which Torontonians traditionally start planting their gardens. To celebrate this, and spring and the end of the long, cold, mushy winter, Bronwyn and her housemates decided to have a concert. The concert took place in the backyard around the rickety wooden steps to the kitchen, and as everyone was in one way or another musical, a mellow sound was made and the neighbors didn't complain too much.

Bronwyn hadn't seen the stranger arrive, but by the time the musicians were ready to pause for drinks, he'd been leaning up against the side of the house awhile. "Stay for a beer?" She called after him as he strolled back towards the road. That was her first encounter with Roy.

The next time he came he brought his harmonica and stayed up half the night jamming. The other half he spent on the couch in the living room, and in the morning he helped Bronwyn plant tomato and sunflower seedlings. "I was raised on a farm," he told her, "but I've always been ashamed of it."

He seemed shy of holding or even touching her at first, until one evening, on a walk, he broke down and cried, and she sat on a park bench with his head in her lap, stroking his hair, and he talked. "He hadn't told me anything up to then," she told Annette, not even his last name. "That's when he said what he did about you."

Annette was doing her best not to cry herself. She'd hardly touched her food, and kept blowing her nose. She remembered lying on her back in Central Park—they'd rented bikes—with

Roy's head on her stomach, looking up through the trees at the sky and wishing the moment could last for ever.

"He said everyone he touched he contaminated, and he didn't want it to happen to me."

"Did he tell you what was the matter?"

"Not specifically. It was about people he trusted letting him down, that he'd never trust himself to trust anyone again type of thing. He said he had to choose between destroying someone's life or destroying his own."

"Did he say who?"

"No."

"Someone he cared for?"

"Yes, from the way he talked."

"Did he mean suicide, do you think?" That letter to Shane, surely wasn't the work of a would-be suicide.

"Not like shooting himself. I guess there are other ways of self-destruction. I told him the story of St. Eulogius of Cordoba. He said he could identify with him."

"I missed that one," Annette flipped back through the hagiography of her Catholic childhood. "How does it go?"

"He was this ninth century priest living in Moorish Spain. In Cordoba things were pretty much in balance between the religions, but an extremist element in the Church needed a martyr, and Eulogius fit the role. He went about proselytizing until his bishop, who was a moderate, feared a backlash and turned him over to the Moors who jailed him. When they let him out, he went right on stirring things up and even took in a young Moslem apostate, Leocritia. This was the last straw. All hell broke loose and in the end they were executed and became saints."

"I see. Roy the martyr. Did he explain?" Bronwyn shook her head. "No clues?"

"Just the feeling he thought he'd been hung out to dry, I guess. He's all right, isn't he?" She could contain asking no longer.

"Last I heard he was in Maryland, on the Chesapeake. Then he disappeared."

"He said he was going away. He didn't say where. I hope everything's worked out."

"Worked out?"

"Something he said the last time I saw him. He was real excited. Like a cloud had lifted. He said if things worked out, he'd a chance to make a new start."

With you, thought Annette. What was it that had suddenly perked him up? Knowing Roy as she'd come to over the past few days, it was a five letter word beginning with M, though she wasn't about to sully the airwaves with it in front of Bronwyn. Visions of Roy trying to fast talk some blood-soaked drug cartel as he searched frantically in a Spanish phrasebook crossed her mind. Suddenly it seemed not improbable that he *was* dead.

"Are you all right?" Bronwyn's hand touched her wrist, her eyes were large with concern. How Roy would have lapped it up. Toss a little Latin into the pot, an obscure saint or two, the backyard music, the kids, the beer, a heady mix. A few minutes ago she was taking a bow at the opera. Now she'd as good as buried the guy.

"Daydreaming." She managed a smile, but Bronwyn wasn't convinced.

"I really do care for him," she said simply, "and that means he's all yours. I can see you care just as much."

Martyrdom, thought Annette, is catching.

Leaving the restaurant, they passed a little red and yellow shrine in an alcove. Annette felt in her purse and added a half roll of lifesavers to the bowl of fruit beside it. Quickly, so Bronwyn wouldn't see. *If things worked out.* Sitting back in her taxi, bound for the hotel through the still sunlit city, Annette knew what she had to do: find Roy before he destroyed himself. But first—acting on Kjelborg's hint—she had a ten o'clock appointment to keep in the morning at the headquarters of the Toronto Metropolitan Police, on College Street.

Detective sergeant Flora MacFaddin was one of those people who inspire confidence as soon as they open their mouths. Many an unwary criminal, Annette surmised, had eaten out of the very hand she was now shaking, the hand that would shoot the bolt on the jailhouse door. Perhaps it was the Scots accent combined with cool, green eyes that seemed to hide no guile. "How are you?" Flora MacFaddin sounded as if she really wanted to know. Annette hadn't expected a woman.

Visitor's pass in hand, they took the elevator to the fourth floor. Annette's impression of the place—from the street—was of a gleaming, low-slung, crouching mosque-like structure, reminiscent of a visit she'd paid to Istanbul with Colin. The fourth floor had the muffled feel of a sleek corporate headquarters. Impersonal, well-tended plants, people peering into monitors, family snapshots on desks, soft lighting. The detective, in a summery coat and skirt boasting a loud stripe, sailed, chin up, across the pile carpet, Annette in her wake. Hardly a uniform in sight. The sign, HOMICIDE & MISSING PERSONS, might have been a joke.

"I suppose I am still a bit of an anomaly around here," MacFaddin said from the far side of a very clean desk, when Annette voiced her surprise. She had braced herself for some macho, gum-chewing brush-off artist. "Ten years ago there weren't any full-fledged female detectives on the force, let alone in Homicide. I was a trainee. I considered myself lucky to get the assignment. We're not a town, even today, that goes in much for murder."

"The Kristi Aranda case?"

"Isn't that why you're here?"

"So you're familiar with it?"

"To put it mildly." MacFaddin rocked back in her chair. "It's carved in tablets of stone between my ears. Raking through the ashes, wondering what we missed, what connections we didn't make. Works better than counting sheep." She looked speculatively at Annette. "Do I take it that you didn't remarry, Mrs Warrender?"

The question surprised her with its assumption. "Well, no, you're right. I didn't."

"And you're not in touch with your former husband at all?"

"Not since he left. I guess I'd like to be. That's really why I'm here."

"Why—do you mind my asking?—would you want to be back in touch?"

"Well," Annette felt herself redden, "I heard he was in trouble. I guess to see if I could help."

"What sort of trouble, Mrs Warrender?"

"Seems he's vanished, owing a lot of money." She explained about the phone call from Baffle and her subsequent visit to Scientists Cliffs.

"Why come to Toronto, if he's not here, and why, specifically, to us?"

Annette hesitated. MacFaddin jumped up. "Tea? Good show, won't be a mo."

Left alone in the small room with its pair of shoved-together desks, and commendatory plaques on the walls, Annette pondered whether coming here had been a wise move. Wouldn't this raking up the past do Roy more harm than good? She'd about decided that it would, when MacFaddin reappeared with a tray.

"Biscuit?" She pushed a packet across the desk.

Annette reached out, saw they were Digestives—a favorite of Colin's—and changed her mind.

"Can't blame you. My American friends swear they're mushed up cardboard."

What would Colin make of this little scene? The thought of his total incomprehension buoyed her. No more trimming her sails to inimical winds, she reminded herself. "It's kind of embarrassing to admit," she said, and watched the detective lean back encouragingly in her chair, "though I've not seen or tried to contact Roy since he walked out on me, I guess I never really got over him, just couldn't admit it. Am I crazy?"

"No more so than most of us," MacFaddin said quietly, hands linked behind her head, elbows jutting like wings.

"I heard he was mixed up somehow with this murder, with the family. I wanted to lay that particular ghost to rest, find out what really happened."

"Mixed up is one way of putting it. He was arrested and charged."

"So I gather. It was pretty hard to take in."

"And you've been in touch with people here about it?"

"Actually, it was his second wife, Selena, who suggested I come; said that Roy's friend, Kjelborg, best man at both our weddings, could probably fill me in."

"Name sounds familiar. And did he?"

Annette recounted their visit to the Queen Street West apartment. "Seems inconceivable, Roy being charged with murder. At least the Roy I knew."

"I had the same feeling: this man couldn't strangle a kitten. You know she was strangled. It takes surprising strength to do that where a strong, healthy eighteen-year-old is concerned."

"Is the case still open?"

"Very much so. We've no statute of limitation on murder here." She leaned forward, hands cradling her tea mug. "I'll get maximum pleasure in nailing the son of a bitch who killed Kristi. The day is like yesterday. Early November, Halloween had come and gone. Eight-thirty at night, the call came in. Three of us in the squad car, Erskine, O'Malley and me—bless their hearts, both now retired.

"Rich girl, slumming in sleazy neighborhood. The papers lapped it up. The boyfriend found her. Ran out on the street yelling blue murder. There were three apartments over a laundromat. Kristi had Number 3. Her door gave onto more stairs leading to her space which was the whole top floor. Numbers 1 and 2 were below her, on either side. She was lying on the bed between the windows.

"Whoever it was, she let him in. The street level door wasn't locked, the buzzer didn't work. But the door to Number 3 had a working lock and a peephole, and Kristi was security conscious we were told. Lucky for the boyfriend, he had an alibi. Had his plane from Paris not been six hours late, as likely as not he'd be in the Don Jail as we speak."

"Was she raped?"

"There are things we can't disclose, things we saw that only the killer could know about. Some day, it'll be those things that will trip him up and put him away for life."

"How about the stepfather?"

"Supposedly on his yacht in Bermuda. Though there's been no reliable independent corroboration."

"And her neighbors?"

"Number 2 was vacant. The Number 1 tenant deaf as a post, and old. In fact, she died very recently. We painted all over for prints. Kristi had had a party a couple of weeks before and we spent months interviewing everyone. You get a feel for who you're looking for, a sixth sense. Like being a casting director, I suppose, and the perfect candidate walks into the room. You *know*."

"Was Roy at the party?"

"It was a younger crowd."

"Her family must be desperate."

Annette sensed an underlying defensiveness. "It's understandable, not wanting to keep the wound open, the twins and so on. They made it clear they'd prefer it to quietly fade away. At the same time, if he's killed once, he could kill again. It's a waiting game. And nine times out of ten a killer talks. It's a need they have."

"Well, thanks so much for taking the time. I'm sure you have things to do."

"Thank *you* for stopping by. Actually, there may just be something. I don't know if you noticed our sign coming in. Hard to miss. I wear two hats here. What we lack in murders, we make up in missing persons, by the thousands. You said your former husband had vanished. Let's see if he's been reported missing. A quick call should do it." She picked up the phone. "Janet, hi. Do me a favor and check the file. Warrender, first name Roylance"— glancing at Annette—"The past few months." She hung up. "So the lawyer told you he owed big bucks?"

Before she could answer the phone pinged. "June? Yep. Perfect."

"Amazing," was all Annette could muster, it had happened so fast.

"If anything turns up, would you like me to be in touch?"

"Please. Just the chance to talk things through with him, one on one. He'll have to face the music, of course, but there's got to be a life beyond that."

FAX THREE

Send to: SURGE, LONDON
Sender: IN VESTIGIUM, INC., NEW YORK

August 31st
Your reaction to our initial reports is understandable, but,
we think, premature. It is too soon for a judgement call, as
we think you will agree if you read on. And by curtailing or
cancelling the Obs's access to credit, you would make it that
much harder to keep tabs on her. (Besides eliminating a
prime source of evidence, should it come to that.) While the
Albanian Connection—your term—at first blush did point to—
again your words—a transfer of allegiance (and why, indeed,
should you continue to bankroll an affair involving a multi-
millionaire?) we now feel that there is more going on here
than meets the eye.

To return for a moment to Soren Gustavus Kjelborg,
a.k.a Ottawa Man, a preliminary check reveals the following.
A dual U.S./Canadian citizen, he is married, without children. His wife, an invalid, is confined to their home in Edina,
a well-to-do suburb of Minneapolis. She suffers from kidney
disease and is dependent on a dialysis machine. If Kjelborg
has an office outside his home, we have not found it; but
judging by the business cards in his possession, his line of
work involves ecology and environmental protection.

The morning after their fish dinner, Kjelborg and the Obs took a twenty-minute tramcar ride out to a rundown part of Toronto. They appeared to be searching for something and, according to a store owner, asked directions to a laundromat. They then took a cab to an affluent part of town where they cruised around, apparently still searching, with Kjelborg directing the driver. The cab left the Obs at the University of Toronto campus and drove off with Kjelborg still inside.

The Obs entered a university building where medieval studies is taught. We waited until she emerged before making enquiries. Apparently she was looking for the girlfriend of her son, who had supposedly mistreated the young lady. Not knowing her name, only that she was a student, the Obs put a sign on the noticeboard: To Whom it May Concern. Urgent. Call Warrender, adding her number at the hotel.

Question: does the Obs have a son, perhaps by the marriage you told us about? There is an R. C. Warrender in the Toronto directory; the son or the ex-husband? The number has been disconnected. Coincidentally, or perhaps not, the address listed is in the same complex as the Frampton apartment. We were told by one of the doormen—with a faint curling of the upper lip—that Mr Warrender moved out "some months ago."

Yesterday evening, at a Vietnamese restaurant, the Obs met with a young woman who appeared to be a stranger (the son's girlfriend?) because, while waiting, she confused her with one of the watchers. Because of this we thought it prudent not to enter the restaurant, a small and uncrowded one. On her way out, she seemed shaken, as if the recipient of bad news.

Before flying home today, the Obs visited Toronto's Police Headquarters, where she had a short private interview in the office of a detective sergeant from the Homicide & Missing Persons Unit.

As indicated above, this is not quite the case we thought it was shaping up to be. No doubt somewhere along the line we will find the key that unlocks all the doors, and—unless we hear from you otherwise—will continue to probe.

CHAPTER THIRTEEN

Back in New York, Annette felt deflated. Still no sign of Colin. Strangely, she had the sensation of already moving out of his orbit. But where on earth was she headed? By what distant star should she plot her course? Planet Roy, after the excitement of the past few days, seemed to have vanished to the dark side of the sun. She turned on the TV, and turned it off again. She looked in the fridge and ordered pizza. She thought of Kjelborg, and realized she still didn't know his full name or where he lived. For all his jollity, she'd sensed a sadness in him. On an impulse, she delved in her purse, came up with his number and dialed. Number disconnected. Finally, she called her three friends and set up a coffee kvetch for the following day.

Walking in after an early morning visit to her supermarket, Annette dumped the shopping for the kvetch on the kitchen table. At that precise moment, the phone rang. The voice at the other end made her feel stronger and safer. "Annette? Flora MacFaddin. Do you mind if I call you that?" Without pausing for an answer, she went on, "Something's come up that might be of interest, but don't put too much stock in it. Your mention that Warrender had a copy of *Spanish for Travelers* with him in Maryland gave me an idea. We alerted our opposite numbers in a few of the countries down south. Well the Belize police responded. Their morgue is in custody of a body that answers Warrender's description. One problem, though. Annette, are you with me?"

"Yes. A body, you said."

"It's simple: no fingers, no prints. Severed, every one. We actually have his prints on file here. I checked. But we're stymied. This is where you come in."

"You want me to—" She couldn't say it.

"Exactly, identify the body. I know you're a busy woman, and believe me I wouldn't ask if I could think of a better way. Of course, I'd go with you. Shouldn't take but a day or two."

"Belize, you said?"

"On the coast south of Mexico."

"Well, I guess so. Yes, why not?"

"Then I'll make the arrangements. Today's Tuesday. Could we make it tomorrow?"

"Um, sure." She made it to the bathroom just in time.

Annette held her audience spellbound as she touched on the comings and goings of her past few weeks. At times they growled at Roy, at times at Baffle, at times they shook their heads in amazement, and at times their eyes misted over and they smiled. Not one of them took to Kjelborg. Jadwiga said he reminded her of a page-turner in Vladivostok who liked his pianists décolleté and became so engrossed in the depths of a bosom that they had to stamp on his foot to get him to turn the page. On Colin, the general consensus was that he'd acted like a spoiled brat.

Two hours into the jollity, the phone rang. "Oh my goodness," Annette exclaimed, flustered, "I tried calling you. They said the number was disconnected."

"Our hearts beat as one, my dear. Whistle and I shall come unto you. As it happens I'm in town for a day or two and owe you a dinner."

"Could we make that a very early one?" Annette said, aware of the sudden hush in the room behind her. They arranged to meet on the steps of the Metropolitan Museum of Art.

"Right you are, Sweetheart. Oh, by the way," he said before hanging up, "if you still have that bit of bumf you mentioned—the one with the logo—bring it along."

"My dear, you're blushing," remarked Jadwiga.

Standing on the topmost step of the museum, Annette surveyed the colorful crowd that spilled down towards Fifth Avenue. They sat, they stood, they sauntered, they sweated in the late afternoon heat. Kjelborg's distinctive size and shape was sure to stand out. Either he hadn't arrived—she was early—or he was waiting in the cool of the building's lobby for the appointed minute. Away to her right, on a bench under some trees, she saw Winifred, Josie and Jadwiga, who'd insisted on escorting her. While not discouraging them, she'd made them promise to behave.

Below her a mime was doing his shtik. Latching on to some innocent passer-by he would copycat their every mannerism to the cruel delight of the crowd. As her eyes roved over the scene in a watchful arc, a yellow cab pulled up to the curb and waited. Kjelborg? she wondered, but whoever it was took their time.

Soon the mime strolled over and leaned a languid elbow on the cab's roof, stifling a yawn. He was consulting an imaginary watch when the rear door opened and—yes—Kjelborg, with a small bag and an umbrella, struggled forth. The mime clapped, his audience followed suit, and the cab moved off leaving Kjelborg center stage. Baffled, he cast around for an explanation. Seeing the mime looking equally baffled, he raised the little hat he was wearing, took a bow and marched up the steps, proffering it left and right. On reaching Annette, with a "May I have the pleasure?" he took her arm. As he replaced his hat and they walked away coins tumbled about his shoulders and tinkled to the ground. The crowd—fickle as crowds can be—clapped and cheered, while the mime was left ignominiously scrabbling for nickels and dimes on the steps.

"You were fabulous," Annette said, extricating her arm and trying to steer Kjelborg away from the bench where sat her friends.

"Broke my heart to chuck all that cash, but there's the principle of the thing, no?"

"There's a little Russian place a block away on Madison." She pointed.

"Lead on, tovarich, or should one say, gospozha?" The sky was the color of mushroom soup, humidity in the nineties. The jacket of Kjelborg's tropical suit was damp all down his spine. In the narrow restaurant, where to stow the bag became a problem. He ended up sliding it between his chair and the wall. It crossed Annette's mind that, as in old times, he expected to crash with her. They ordered tea and a plate of piroshki.

"I followed your suggestion to check with the police. Turns out the Missing Persons squad has had a report on file on Roy since June. I'd mentioned about finding the Spanish phrase book and they put out an alert to a few places. Belize responded. They need someone to identify a body in the morgue. I'm going down there tomorrow."

"A body? To Belize?" He seemed astonished. "Don't they speak English there?"

"It seems like a long shot, I know."

Kjelborg stirred the jam in the bottom of his tea. "Not as long as you might think, perhaps."

She glanced up to see if he was serious.

"My dear, I have a confession to make. Roy, God love him, owed a fortune to the wrong crowd; the sort that don't sit around discussing debt refinancing. Scared shitless, he was, if you'll pardon the expression. So he came to me. I told you we were on the outs. We were. Needed to skip town temporarily, he said, and resurface where the rainbow ends smelling sweeter than Shirley Temple, and everyone would be oh so happy. I told him what he needed was more a damn good hiding than a hiding place. But I found him Scientists Cliffs, and a few weeks later had him plucked off the beach and loaded onto a south-bound banana boat. And that was that. Exit Roy, trumpets and alarums off." As if on cue came the rumblings of an approaching storm.

Annette looked at him with new eyes. "I'm impressed."

"You are?" Kjelborg's hangdog features rearranged themselves into a smile. "In that case I deem the whole escapade worthwhile."

"But what about the car? He had a car down there. The neighbors told me so."

"I came in on the boat and drove off in the car."

"Was it you who tipped off the cops?"

"It was his bright idea: make it look like he left in a hurry. The car was in Roy's name. Abandon it at Dulles to throw them off the scent. Cops and robbers."

The chair was small, the table was small, Kjelborg looked awkward and out of place. Annette couldn't help but feel sorry for him. At a particularly ear-rending blast she wheeled around to face the street, then went and stood by the glass door, trying to digest this news. Kjelborg joined her.

"Blow, winds, and crack your cheeks!" he inveighed. The sky darkened, newsprint and trash wafted by, lured by some invisible Pied Piper. A brief lull, then the rain, straight down into suddenly gushing gutters. A waiter dashed in, wet and shiny, hair and clothes flattened against his skin.

Annette said, "I remember, growing up, the darkness before the summer storms in the tobacco fields at Roy's. And sheltering in the drying barns—the smell, kind of acrid that made my nose twitch—and the feeling of sweet sadness. Those were some of my favorite times. Now and then I'll buy a pack of Dunhills just to sniff, though the effect's not quite the same."

"I'd forgotten how far you and Roy go back," Kjelborg said. The feeling of being marooned in the little restaurant seemed to bring them closer.

"How did you two find each other? You always seemed a bit like the Odd Couple to me."

"Deception played its part, the only two sincerely insincere Lutherans at the seminary. Insincerity loves company, I guess. So we sat out Vietnam in the peat bogs of Northern Minnesota watching *Gilligan's Island* and having fellowship one with another."

"Did you see a big change in Roy between those days and now?"

"Do people really change, after the age of two, I mean? You, for instance. Oh, you present a different face to the world from twenty years ago—self-assured, smart, almost hard I'd say if I didn't know better—but the Annette who was so kind and believing, the Annette essence, that's what still comes through."

They accepted the waiter's offer of more tea. "What is the Annette essence?" she wondered. "I'm sure I don't know."

"Oh, you do, if you're sufficiently ruthless and manage to kick the habit of dishonesty we get hooked on about ourselves; seeing oneself through outside eyes, as it were, and losing the inner sight in our own. On the other hand," he added, "perhaps it's the not seeing that helps to keep one sane."

"I have the strangest feeling," Annette said after a while, "that Roy needs me. And surely, if he needs me, he's alive."

"Suppose he is. Suppose you track him down. Then what? He's going to hate you. Are you ready for that? *Why* is he going to hate you? For confronting him with what he's become."

"He said leaving me was his biggest mistake." Bronwyn had told her.

Kjelborg was unimpressed. "But that's my point. *His biggest mistake.* That's what he'll see when he sees you. That's why he'll hate you."

She wished she hadn't brought the subject up. "Oh, I have that bit of paper you wanted." She searched in her bag.

Kjelborg held it at arm's length to the light. "Blasted feline. Gorgonzola, my arse," he mumbled, before stashing it in his pocket.

"Why is it so important?"

"It isn't, any more."

"So it was you who trashed the place at Scientists Cliffs?"

"Trashed? I was looking for this," he patted his jacket pocket, "and anything else that would link me to Roy. It was the middle of the night. I was in a hurry."

"I'll say."

"The cops will have done their bit." He glanced over Annette's shoulder at the street and signaled for the check. "No, this one's on me. Unless they've picked my pocket again." It was still raining but not as heavily, and the sky was brighter. The storm had moved on.

Kjelborg paid and asked for directions to the men's room. Picking up his bag, he moved towards the rear of the restaurant. He doesn't trust me, that's for sure, Annette thought, amused. The minutes ticked by. The rain stopped. The sun came out. Kjelborg was taking his time. "Is my friend back there?" she asked the waiter. "I hope he's not sick or something."

The waiter returned, shaking his head.

"Is there another way out?"

He shrugged. "Only kitchen."

"Did he leave through the kitchen?"

"But it's not possible."

"Could you check."

When the waiter returned he didn't know whether to smile or frown, and tried both. "Ten minutes ago, your friend, he is passing through kitchen."

Kjelborg's umbrella was hanging where he'd left it. She grabbed it and walked out.

CHAPTER FOURTEEN

Miami Airport. Squeezing by a pair of straining tights depicting various colorful fruits, Annette made her way through the home-bound holiday throng. Had she worn her leopardskin leotards she'd have been right in style. Gold sandals, flashy jewelry, lips in luscious reds. Already the exotic blood in her veins was tingling. Yet she was going to view a corpse. She shivered imagining standing with MacFaddin in a clammy chamber, a man in a white coat pulling out a coffin-size drawer—the way she'd seen it done on TV, one glance sufficing. But suppose it wasn't a simple yes or no and the features had deteriorated beyond recognition, quite likely in a hot climate. What then? Dental charts crossed her mind. She wondered vaguely who Roy's dentist was, or even if he had one. He'd always hated going.

"Your purse too please, Señorita!"

Annette watched her hand baggage being fed into the x-ray machine. She'd packed clothes for a week, just in case, and left a note for Colin on the kitchen table in the unlikely event he'd turn up: *Darling, I'm off to Belize for a few days R & R.* Unsigned. Recognition & Retrieval, in this case. God, if he only knew! Once through Security, she made for the gate to meet up with Mac-Faddin, flying in from Toronto.

"Over here!" called an unmistakeable voice. In a light yellow raincoat, she was at a counter sending a grapefruit gift package to her mother-in-law. "She could buy the same damn things at her corner greengrocers, three for a dollar, but it's the thought that counts, right?"

"Would you like them individually personalized?" asked the clerk.

"Sure, monogram the lot. Have you noticed, nobody speaks English any more?" she asked Annette as they moved to the waiting area. "I keep wondering why—if it *is* him—Belize. I'm not sure they even speak Spanish. Of course there's the ganja, quite a hot spot, I gather. Bunch of off-shore islands, ideal for smuggling, and they grow the stuff too. Quality, I'm told. Would he be involved in that?"

"Oh, no," said Annette. Then, recalling her thoughts in the Vietnamese restaurant, "Well, I can't imagine—"

"Out with it."

"It's just that, according to a friend of his I met in Toronto, he seemed really down. Then, right before he disappeared, he brightened up. If things work out, he said. And that just stuck in my mind. As if he had some scheme or other up his sleeve to get out from under his debt."

Should I tell her about Kjelborg? flashed through her mind. He wouldn't thank her for it, she was sure. And besides, what difference would it make? Though his abrupt exit from the restaurant the previous day irked and puzzled her.

An announcement was coming over the PA system. They weren't calling the flight, they were asking Detective sergeant MacFaddin to step up to the counter. Annette noted several pairs of eyes following the yellow raincoat as she threaded her way between the seats. She saw her glance at a note and head towards a bank of phones. After two or three minutes on the phone, she started back towards Annette, who did her best to glean a message from that implacably neutral gaze.

"Well, troops, about turn."

"What?"

"Marching orders. That was Toronto. The dear old Belize police were on the blower, egg on their collective face. The body's gone missing. No body, no trip. The digit-less one has apparently vanished. Prestidigitation, no doubt. Now," she turned businesslike, "if you've any bags checked, I suggest we try to liberate them pronto. For myself, I travel light."

"You mean someone stole it?"

"It didn't leave on its own accord, I gather."

"So it probably wasn't Roy?"

"That's one possibility, I grant you."

"Supposing I go without you?" Annette quite surprised herself. "I was kind of looking forward to a bit of a break."

"Can't blame you. You've come this far, why not?"

While MacFaddin went to sort out her ticket, Annette did some sorting of her own. An unlikely feeling, like elation, had invaded her—the sensation she remembered as a teenager the one time she did some mushroom. She couldn't have stood up if she'd been ordered to. After all the beating around the bush, the crying in the dark, at last she seemed to hear a response, an echo, the merest rustle in the undergrowth. What had Kjelborg said? A south-bound banana boat. The yellow raincoat was heading back.

A 'last and final call' over the PA system urged all remaining passengers for Belize to board the aircraft immediately. It was time to go. MacFaddin scrawled something on the back of a business card. "My Belize police contact," she said. "Feel free to look him up. May come in useful. You never know."

FAX FOUR

Send to: SURGE, LONDON
Sender: IN VESTIGIUM, INC., NEW YORK

September 2nd

On Tuesday morning the Obs entertained three women friends at the apartment, then accompanied them to the Metropolitan Museum of Art. Leaving the friends on a bench under some trees, she climbed to the top step and stood by the door, apparently on the lookout for someone. Who should get out of a cab on Fifth Avenue with a small suitcase but Ottawa Man, a.k.a. Soren Gustavus Kjelborg.

He seemed in good spirits, playing along with a mime who was working the crowd. Even getting a round of applause as he greeted the Obs and, arm in arm, walked back down the steps with her. They proceeded to a nearby restaurant on Madison Avenue, trailed inexpertly by the three friends. Ottawa Man seemed uncomfortably aware of this escort.

While the trio lingered uncertainly under an awning across the avenue from the restaurant, our watcher waited at a convenience store a few doors away. With a thunderstorm threatening, the trio dispersed. Just before the storm broke, a man with a heavy accent, who proved to be a waiter from the (Russian) restaurant, entered the store and bought whipping cream. A cash donation secured his eyes and ears for an hour.

When the storm passed, our watcher took a stroll. The Obs's table was near the door. She sat alone. After ten minutes, she left by herself. According to the waiter, her companion had exited through the kitchen onto a side street and the Obs had seemed surprised. He took his bag but not his umbrella. Asked what they had talked about, the waiter said, tobacco.

Next morning, Monday, the Obs boarded a flight at La-Guardia for Miami. At Miami International, she transferred to a flight to Belize.

On arrival in Belize City, the Obs took a taxi to the Fort George Hotel, virtually the only luxury hotel in town, and checked into a single room.

We will proceed with the investigation along the original guidelines unless we receive contrary, or additional, instructions.

CHAPTER FIFTEEN

Annette lost little time at the Fort George. She dumped her things in the room (MacFaddin had made the reservation) and glanced out the window—a road, the sea, a ship or two riding at anchor. She touched up her face, anointed her underarms, and sallied forth into what was left of the steamy afternoon. A cab waited conveniently at the curb. "The Police Station, please." Kjelborg was right, they spoke English. Apart from that, for all she knew about this place, she might have landed on the moon.

Nor had her ride from the airport whetted her appetite to learn more. Belize City seemed to her a mess, a town planner's nightmare. Erratic paving, crumbling buildings, fetid waterways, broken-down vehicles, dirty, tired, noisy people. Had coming here been a big mistake, a spur of the moment wrong call? As the cab clanked to a halt in the middle of the road, Annette—searching in her purse for the card MacFaddin had given her—finally found it: *Please give Mrs Warrender all possible assistance.* She looked up. "Peleeze Stashun," the driver announced laconically.

Steps led up to a low-slung whitish building, out of one of Colin's Graham Greene colonial backwater novels. "I'm afraid I'm new here. Just off the plane from New York."

"Doan tell me." He didn't look round. "We a sayin' here in Belize: De fasta you go, de sooner you get dere." He pointed heavenwards. "Sooner or later everybody laan."

"Very nice," said Annette, producing a fistful of local currency and missing the point. "How much?"

"Fi' dollah de ride. Advice free. Doan give profeshnal help."

Inside the station a knock-kneed constable marched her down a passage and across a yard. He pounded on a door that said SPECIAL BRANCH and left her.

"Mrs Warrender, please come in." A crisp young man in an open neck white shirt, creased white slacks and blue suede shoes ushered her though a desk-cluttered antechamber into a small office, waved her to a chair and adjusted a fan. The breeze helped. A sign on the desk said, ELVIS P. RUIZ. "How's Toronto?"

"Actually, I'm from New York," Annette responded, a little winded by this sudden rush of ease when she'd anticipated more of a battering ram type approach.

"But you *are* Mrs Warrender?" He smiled. His teeth matched his outfit, his skin was deep gold, his hair curly and black, and his eyelashes so long and perfectly formed that on a woman she'd have suspected they were false.

"And *you* are a cop?" Could that P possibly stand for—? She produced MacFaddin's card.

"In fact, three years ago, I took a course up there, perhaps why I was assigned this case. The detective sergeant has been on the phone. I was waiting for you." He glanced at a clock on the wall that showed a little after five. "I should first of all apologize for the mix-up. It's embarrassing for us, and most painful, I'm sure, for you."

"You know I'm just the first wife?" she put in to stem the flow of sympathy. "It's been twenty years."

"Detective sergeant MacFaddin explained everything."

"So what exactly happened?"

Ruiz pulled a sheaf of notes towards him. "Let me confess, I only got the case this morning. The police were handling it up to then." No egg on my face.

"Aren't you the police?"

"We're Special Branch. More like your FBI or RCMP. We handle anything that spills over our national borders. Are you familiar with our geography, Mrs Warrender?" Standing tiptoe he pulled down a map on the wall behind him. Cracked and yellowed, it took her back to high school and Miss Maberley, the social studies teacher.

"I know we're two hours flying time south of Miami, and I guess that's the Caribbean out there."

"It's out of date, as you see. We're no longer British Honduras. We've been independent ten years now." With a ruler, Ruiz touched a point close to the western border. "That's where his car was found."

"Car?"

"Yes. It was in all the papers."

"Not in New York, it wasn't. All I know is, there was a body in the morgue here that might have been Roy." She peered again at the point Ruiz indicated. "The brown bits, are those mountains?"

"More like foothills."

"But isn't that the middle of nowhere. What would Roy be doing there?"

"It all seem pretty run o' the mill at the time, Mrs Warrender. A tourist. An accident. It happens. The caves up there can be treacherous. Only when word come from Toronto about a missing person, the police put two and two together. A white man's corpse, incognito, in the morgue. They jump to the conclusion—leap maybe—it's him. That's when we got the case."

"This missing tourist. Wasn't he identified?"

"Maybe he paid cash. You'll find we're a little bit laid back down here, Mrs Warrender, by New York standards. That's just the way we like it." He thumbed through some notes. "There was an overnight bag in the trunk: change of clothes, toiletries, nothing unusual. In the back seat: umbrella, yellow rain slicker."

"You have that?"

"Police haven't turned it over yet. No sign of struggle inside or outside of vehicle." He read on, then leaned over and twiddled the combination on a floor safe at his feet. "This is all they give me." He dumped the contents of a bulging folder onto the desk. A chunk of stone fell out, quartz-like, with a yellowish brown stain along one edge.

"That's not blood, is it?"

Ruiz hefted it. "Ah, the murder weapon?" He smiled. "More likely a souvenir. No cash, no driver license, no credit cards." He held up a folded map and a slip of paper fell out.

"What's that?"

"A bar receipt from the San Ignacio Inn," he read, "made out to a C. McKenzie: Two Belikin, 4.50 BZ dollars. Paid cash. That's the nearest town, to where the car was found, San Ignacio."

"Can I see?" Her hand shook so much, she could scarcely read. "It's him," she said, "Calvin."

"You know him?"

"It's Roy. I knew it. I sensed it." *Kjelborg & McKenzie.* Oh boy. So this was where the rainbow ended? In a yellow slicker. In a cave. In Belize. The idea was ridiculous, surreal. She felt like laughing.

Ruiz shuffled through his notes. "Yes, here we are. A Mr. Calvin McKenzie. Stayed at the San Ignacio Inn around that time. No forwarding address."

He stood up smartly, brushed himself off, and jabbed again at the map on the wall. What had started out as a major embarrassment, to be buried as quickly as possible, showed signs of becoming a career-enhancing opportunity. "Ten to one, if he's alive he's in Guatemala." He beckoned Annette up for a closer look. "Here's where the car was found, see? Maybe ten miles—as the crow flies mind you—to the border. I tell you, he's in Guatemala."

"You mean he could just walk across?"

"I grant you, he have a devil of a job walking anywhere in that jungle. Up and down, up and down, see all the streams? And the snakes, man, they sting you from behind, you're dead before you know it. The only ones that move through there are the army patrols."

Annette stared at the map. "There seem to be a number of villages."

"Logging camps. Deserted long ago. Dots on the map."

"You really think he made it out?"

"Show me the body. They search the whole area."

"What about the one in the morgue?"

"Ganja business, ten to one."

Annette couldn't conceive of her Roy, however desperate, footing it through the jungle to Guatemala given any other way to get there. Besides, he had a phobia of snakes. The closest to wildlife he'd get, outside of the box, was the Central Park Zoo. "So what do we do?"

Ruiz shrugged. "Nothing."

"But—"

"What crime has the man committed?"

She opened her mouth, shut it, re-opened it. "That's it?" She couldn't hide her disappointment.

"Mrs Warrender, be reasonable. What did you expect? Try to see things from our side. Down here it's not a crime to disappear. In fact, it's an art form. Some folk come just for that."

"OK, so I'm just his first wife. We had very few years together, but I'd known him since he was fifteen. How often does the first wife get a second chance? If he's alive, I want to find him. Maybe help him."

"What's the time in Toronto now, Mrs Warrender? A bit after seven, right?" Ruiz picked up the office phone and dialed.

Out on the street daylight was fast giving way to dusk. Annette decided to walk back to her hotel. She needed time alone with herself. It couldn't be more than a few blocks, and if she headed back the way the taxi had come she'd get her bearings. Just as well MacFaddin hadn't picked up her phone. Ruiz left a brief message for the morning.

People were all around, vehicles jockeyed for position. In shops, here and there, lights were coming on. She walked slowly, picking her way over the uneven sidewalk past open drains, glad for her low heels, feeling a gradual loosening in mind and body from all the tension of the day. Here she was in this foreign town among ordinary people struggling to squeeze a little living between making a living. She mustn't be too hard on the place. Who was she to judge and condemn, who—by no sweat of her own, just the use of a rectangular bit of plastic—could command so much. As for Special Branch Officer Elvis P Ruiz, what had she expected him to do exactly? Wasn't it enough that he too thought Roy alive, though in a neighboring country. Perhaps he's right.

Funny, she didn't remember a bridge. Ahead people were thronging, waiting, traffic at a standstill as the two halves of a swing bridge jerked into the blue-gray sky. Confused, she re-traced her steps, hurrying now out of a frisson of fear. Had the taxi come from the left and she hadn't noticed the turn? She struck off down a side street that seemed vaguely familiar. Yet, how could it be? At an intersection she peered about, down streets—alleys really—even dingier than the one she was on.

"Anyting I can do to help?"

The timing of the offer and its gentle, earnest delivery, quelled the panic that an unseen voice, so close at hand, might have triggered. Though when she turned, her worst fears were realized. His shorts and tank top revealed bulging brown mus-cles, his hair writhed Medusa-like from his head, his eyes bored into hers. "That's all right," she said instinctively, tightening her grasp on her purse in a way she hoped wouldn't give offense.

"I tink mebbe you was loss."

"I'm returning to my hotel," she said, attempting to sound purposeful. How often had she cautioned visitors back home to look like they knew where they were going.

"De Fart Jarge is dat?"

"Yes." She marched off. How did he know? What she should have said was, Mind your own business.

"Fart Jarge over dis way, lady. Better I tek you."

To about-turn now would be to deliver herself into the clutches of this wild-looking person. Stumbling blindly on would probably lead to a similar fate. Chances were, by going along, she could keep him sweet until the time came to safely ditch him. "Oh, right," she said, as if remembering, "just point me in the general direction. I'll find my way."

"Waakin' de street afa dark unsafe for woman aloan. Pro-tekshun from de criminal element, dat wa you need. Woman need man for protekshun," he scolded. "You no man dere wid you?"

"My husband's back at the hotel."

They set off. "Paul, dat's wa dey caal me."

"They call me Annette."

"Where you from in de States, Annette?"

"New York City."

"Dat wat I tink aaready. Nu Yaak. It's de fas' way y' waak. Dey aal do from dere."

"You know a lot." If she could keep up this banter she might be all right.

"I a knowin' saat o' man." Indeed, Paul was hailed by motley types, mostly classifiable by Annette as the criminal element. As they looked her over, she began to feel like a trophy brought back from the wars. "Hey, Pigface!" called out two girls with black, shining faces and elaborately braided hair. Setting out for a night's work, she judged.

Paul's face darkened with annoyance. Clearly, he had other identities. "They're beautiful," she remarked, to cover the moment.

"Why you at de Peleeze Stashun dis afanoon?" His tone was suddenly less than friendly.

He's been shadowing me, had me picked out as a likely hit. Annette shuddered at her innocence. "They were helping me."

"Dey noa helpin' nobody. Yuh wan help, come to a soshal facilitator. Da's me. Tell me de problem. I han' you solushan."

And I hand you cash. "OK." She took a deep breath. "A body is missing from the police morgue, believed stolen."

"Oh, de white man body." A statement, not a question. "Doan worry. I no do dat one meself. But as a knowin' sort o' man, I tell you who did."

"Are you sure you know what I'm talking about?"

"De one wid de han' chop off, no? De human barracuda done dat job."

"The —-?"

"De bruddah call hisself de human barracuda. Wa de peleeze tell you?"

"Not much."

"Doan know piss from shit down dere. In the marnin' I bring de bruddah outside de Fart Jarge."

Which, she realized with a start, was exactly where they'd arrived. The sturdy gates, the guard—she could have hugged him right there in his little kiosk.

"Thanks for showing me the way." She thrust some bills at her guide.

"Wha' dis?" he recoiled.

She added some more and wished him good night.

CHAPTER SIXTEEN

Next morning a muffled figure—headscarf, shades, light rain-coat—could be seen stepping hurriedly between the front door of the Fort George and a waiting taxi, into the trunk of which had been loaded a suitcase. As the taxi crawled through the gate and out past the guard, two men lounging under a palm tree picked themselves up, stared hard at the retreating vehicle, looked at each other, and loped off after it.

From the back seat, Annette watched street life surging beyond the window. When a sudden downpour sent people skipping and ducking for cover, she relaxed enough to take off the headscarf. Was she being ridiculous? The idea of another encounter with the all-knowing Paul, did not appeal. The taxi proceeded cautiously. *Hot Tamales, Bread Pudding*, advertised a hand-painted sign. The rain eased off. Roy, where are you now, this very minute, you old bullshitter?

The desk put through Flora MacFaddin's call at 7 AM. She hadn't yet reached Ruiz. "Well, if you're up for it, I've certainly no objection," she said, when Annette laid out her plan to visit the area where Roy was last known to have been. "You've come up trumps so far, that's for sure. And if Detective Ruiz feels it's no longer his bailiwick, so be it. Let's keep in touch if at all possible. Where will you be tonight?"

"The San Ignacio Inn. Two or three nights perhaps. The desk here's made reservations."

"Bus stashun!" The announcement startled her out of her reverie. The driver pointed. A battered school-type bus stood at the curb, the words BENQUE VIEJO in its window. People milled around and men loaded baggage on the roof.

"That the San Ignacio bus?"

"Dat de one, de 'leven o'clock. Ticket office over dere," indicating a dingy hangout on the corner. "I deal wid de loggage."

"But it says Benque Viejo."

"Benque de las' stop. At de border."

Some minutes and many misgivings later, Annette found herself seated near the back of the crowded bus with her knees level with her chin because the only space she could find was over the wheel. Her bag was on the roof and she'd given up worrying about what would happen if it rained again. The hotel had assured her that—short of renting a car, unappealing in this unpredictable land—the fastest, easiest way to San Ignacio was the bus. And San Ignacio was where she must go, to pick up Roy's trail and try and coax some sense out of the whole tangled mess.

Ruminating thus amid the chatter and bustle and smells, hot and impatient to be off, she gradually became aware of an altercation up front. Necks craned, comments flew and, if she wasn't mistaken, people turned to stare—at her. She looked questioningly at her neighbor.

"No ticket, no admittance, driber say."

A tapping at her window explained everything: Paul, chest heaving, accusing eyes staring; at his back an older, skinnier version of himself, minus the manic energy. The human barracuda? He didn't look to have much bite left in him. "Dis bruddah in de body bisness heart an' soul, Annette, know aal de ins an' outs. Catch de one o'clock, he lay everyting out."

"When I come back," she said, "Don't worry." As if on cue, the bus gave a lurch.

"We waitin' for you," he promised—or threatened—she wasn't sure which. There wasn't much more he could do. The bus was moving. The human barracuda, unseen by Paul, delivered himself of a grave, unfocussed salute.

"Dat man brain so cook he doan know he 'live or dead," the woman beside her remarked.

The coconut pie served up in the dining room of the San Ignacio Inn—a slightly ramshackle but pleasant colonial remnant—had outlasted a Belikin beer and two cups of coffee and Annette still hadn't made an appreciable dent in it. After a late lunch, she'd hoped to press on to the Rio Frio caves, but the taxi man who ferried her up the hill from the town center dissuaded her. No point in hurrying, he said, no place to be stuck in after sundown. A clear four hours of daylight were needed for the round trip. He seemed a knowledgeable sort and she engaged him for the following morning at eight.

All in all, Annette was glad for the break. She'd been on the go since her feet touched Belizean soil, and between the heat and the bus was about ready to collapse. Not that she hadn't—surprisingly—enjoyed being shaken like a martini for two hours with a bunch of Belizeans, in a sort of a group escape from the travails of the city.

Wandering out behind the inn, she looked over a ravine so deep she scarcely glimpsed the river at the bottom. Perhaps the jungle began down there beyond the swimming pool, stretching away as far as the eye could see. She fancied monkeys swinging in the trees and the harsh squawk of parrots. Holding up Roy's map (on loan from Ruiz) she found San Ignacio and—circled in pencil—the Rio Frio caves, bordering Mountain Pine Ridge which merged southward into the Maya Mountains.

The other place circled was Xunantunich, a name she couldn't even begin to pronounce, a place of archeological interest according to the map. Hmmm. She glanced at her watch. It looked right off the Benque road, almost at the border. Folding the map away, an uneasy thought struck her. Why hadn't Roy taken his map? Heading into the back country, as Ruiz suggested, surely he'd need it.

In the Mayan language, the letter *X*—according to the helpful lady at the front desk—is pronounced *sh*: *Shun-an-tun-ich*. A young man, settling his bill, piped up, "Hey, need a ride? We're going right by there." Medical students from New Hampshire, they were driving to Tikal, on the Guatemalan side.

"You've no problem, as tourists, going there?"

"Tourists are generally OK. It's against the law to hunt them down and shoot them. Not that the law carries much weight."

"You're kidding."

"Seriously, stick with a group. Women alone, they get ideas." And a man alone? she wondered. Still, she'd come this far, why not?

They let her off by the roadside and Annette soon found herself being hand-cranked across a river on a creaking ferry. "Keep on de path, ca'an miss," the ferryman directed as she set off down it, shrouded by palm boughs like giant green ostrich feathers blocking out the sky. So quiet, never in her life had she felt so self-aware, like the last person left on earth.

A little later she realized how far from alone she really was: an unbroken line of ants moved across the track each one bearing a tiny bit of leaf like a green umbrella, a fantastic caravan wobbling over the stones. Bending close, she fancied she could hear the faintest rustle down the line. In one spot, where the ground was muddy, they struggled over ridges made by fresh-looking tire treads. Looks like she'd have company.

Sure enough, in a clearing she came upon a mud-splattered camper where trees gave way to grassy meadowland and a band of ragamuffins chased a ball. At either end of the meadow rose the ruins. In a thatched hut, bearing the weighty designation VIS-ITOR CENTRE, an old man bustled about collecting her 3 BZ dollar fee. Flicking back a few pages in the guest book, she came to an entry in familiar writing. Not Roy Warrender: Calvin McKenzie.

From the summit of the smaller ruin—little more than a hill of bush-covered rubble topped by exposed stonework—she gazed out over a wide green valley ringed by low hills. What power those Mayan priests must have felt. Had Roy stood here too, just weeks ago? With what on his mind? Butterflies—large and black with pale green markings, black with blue circles and red tips, bright orange, mottled gray—drifted lazily in the sunshine.

From the direction of the main ruin, which stood out like a castle battlement against the sky, came snatches of voices, carrying American voices: "So much for all the exotic birds mentioned in the guidebook!" Annette, a hundred yards away, could have enlightened them, siblings from Oklahoma named Earl and Virginia she'd encountered at the bar of the Fort George. Nearby, a young soldier in camouflage idly caressed his rifle.

As if on cue, a bevy of snow-white egrets winged overhead perhaps on their way to roost. Time to be heading back myself, she thought. An early night and an early start in the morning. Crossing the river, her one thought was to quench her thirst;

crazy, not to have brought water. A sign, LA CALAVERA DE CRYSTAL RESTAURANT BAR, caught her eye. She entered the tiny lean-to and presently a crone hobbled in from the back. She produced a Seven-up and, with a moment's tell-tale hesitation, stuck in a straw. On a bench in the shade Annette set the straw carefully aside for the next customer, perhaps not as fussy about chewed ends, and watched the strong, active hands of women kneading their washing on flat river rocks. Silently she toasted Roy for bringing her to this unlikely but entrancing spot.

A few minutes later, the pop-up camper inched its way onto the ferry. "Hi there!" Earl leaned out as it climbed the bank towards her. "Need a ride to town?"

FAX FIVE

Send to: SURGE, LONDON
Sender: IN VESTIGIUM, INC., NEW YORK

September 4th

In the late afternoon of her first day in Belize, the Obs lost no time in slipping out of her hotel and was off the radar for a period of two hours. On her return, two watchers fell into conversation with her at the bar. She seemed flushed and excited, and ordered dinner to be sent to her room.

Yesterday, after breakfast, the Obs checked out of the Fort George and took a taxi to the bus station. The hotel had booked her a room at the Inn in San Ignacio, a town near the border with Guatemala. As the bus was about to depart, two individuals of the Rasta persuasion, rebuffed from boarding by the driver, ran round to the Obs's window, appearing to remonstrate with her.

After lunch at the San Ignacio Inn, the Obs visited a ruined Maya temple in the bush not far from the border. According to the caretaker at the Visitor Center, she had paged back through the guest book and appeared interested in one particular entry. He wasn't sure which. The watchers noted the name, S. Kjelborg, with a date just over a year ago. Shown a photo of Ottawa Man, the caretaker, an old but savvy Mayan, said he remembered him clearly.

The Obs accepted a ride back to the San Ignacio Inn with watchers and arranged for them to join her the following morning—this morning—on an excursion into the mountains.

Whatever is afoot, it is our belief that building a trusting relationship with the Obs is the key to finding out.

CHAPTER SEVENTEEN

Annette ate alone that evening and skipped the coconut pie. Earl and Virginia were at a guest house up the road. She was beginning to regret inviting them to join her on the trip to the caves. But—extra pairs of eyes and ears—you never know. She would pay for the cab herself, so they wouldn't have to take the camper.

Voices filtered through from the long bar back of the dining room, one bringing Colin to mind with its Britishness. Once he realized she was gone, would he raise heaven and earth to find her or simply shrug her off? Her spending on the card would drive him nuts when he saw the bill, but what could he do?

"Oh, now you mention it," the man at the bar declared, at Annette's description of Calvin McKenzie. "Odd sort of geezer." He'd likely have recalled Alexander the Great and the Queen of Sheba for a chance to buy a pretty woman a drink; a bachelor eking out retirement on a British Rail pension, she'd discovered. "One of those scavenging Yank business types with an eye to the main chance."

"Friend of a friend," Annette murmured, "just curious about what happened."

"Not devoid of redeeming qualities, I daresay. Swallowed up in a cave, wasn't he? Taken my advice, he'd be drinking today. Chin chin. Should have lined up a qualified speleo-what-you-macall-it before going near the things. Run for miles, I'm told. Now *tunnels...*" As soon as Annette could get away, she borrowed a book from the hotel library about the caves and took it to bed with her. By page three she'd nodded off.

Ascensión Coc pulled up to the inn at 8 AM sharp in a 4-wheel-drive Land Rover borrowed from his brother-in-law, "just to be on the safe side." Virginia and Earl were waiting with a supply of the toothbrushes and snakebite kits they were giving away to clinics. Annette had to admire them. Soon they were bouncing along on a dusty, stoney, curving, gently climbing road, Ascensión bouncing particularly high—the only way he could see over the hood. Like many of his countrymen, he was short, and with his crinkled Hobbit-like demeanor, might be any age between forty and seventy.

They stopped after an hour for a warm Fanta at a wisp of a general store. A sign advertised PIG-TAIL at two dollars a pound. Earl took a photo. Virginia shrieked over a bottle on a shelf: *Woodward's Original Gripe Water*. Earl snapped her pretending to drink it. As I'd feared, thought Annette. A while later they halted at a barrier and a man emerged from a hut. "Forest Reserve begin here," Ascensión explained. The man, in khaki pants and a bush shirt, looked official, kind of. He passed a clipboard through the driver's window. "New regulation," Ascensión apologized. "Aal visitor signing in person now." They signed.

"What was all that about?" Virginia asked when they were through.

"Wan' be sure you outa here by nightfaal. Safety precaation, y'might say. Before I jus' write American, German, French. Now dey wan' whole name. Aal on account of dat tourist gone missing at Rio Frio."

"Tourist, you say? Gone missing!" Virginia piped up over the noise of the engine. "Earl, you hear that? Recently?"

"Some say he still up dere, hidin' out in one of de old loggin' camps."

"What do *you* think?" Annette asked nervously.

Ascensión drove. Hadn't he heard her? The road was rutted, with bits washed away. Pine trees crowded straight and tall on either side. "Mighty queer place dose caves," he said eventually, "nobody know what in dem. Some just go on and on. Who know where dey go?"

In an open area among the pines where a river gushed through a cleft in the rocks, cascading in a series of pools, they made a rest stop. More like the Ozarks than the tropics, Earl remarked. Ascensión picked up a piece of rock. "See this?" he showed Annette. "Granite." Like the chunk in Roy's car. "Aal dis side," his arm embraced the river and the forest behind them, "aal granite. Mountain Pine Ridge. Over dere," he pointed across the river, "de Chiquibul basin, hundreds of miles, aal limestone. At de meetin' point, dat's where you fine de caves."

"Those pools look mighty cool," said Virginia. "I'd sure like to have me a dip."

"Five Tommies drown aaready," Ascensión warned, "De place is deceivin'."

The women climbed up to a hut marked WC. On the way down, Annette just couldn't keep it in. "That tourist that went missing up by the caves," she blurted, "that was my former husband. It's a long story, but that's why I'm here."

Virginia stopped dead. "Well, I'll be— You know what, dearie," she gripped Annette's arm, "I kinda thought there might be something like that, only I didn't like to ask." Annette sketched in some background till Earl leaned out of the Land Rover and yelled for them to hurry.

Leaving the pines behind, they plunged into deep jungle. Annette had a sense of tall trees swaying overhead, hanging vines and fat orchids lolling among the branches. "Is this where the tourist disappeared?" she asked.

"Dey find de car right here, key in ignishun," Ascensión confirmed, bumping to a halt.

"Who did?" Virginia asked, glancing at Annette.

"Workers from de fores' stashun." A desolate collection of huts they'd passed where the road forked. "Go ahead in dere." Ascensión indicated a gap scarcely visible in a thicket of greens and browns. "Jus' follow de path to the cave. Ca'an get loss. I waitin' here."

"I was reading last night that the Mayans thought the caves were the entrance to the underworld where they all come from," Annette whispered as they prepared to set off. "Maybe he's superstitious."

Virginia shivered, "I just had to tell Earl about—you know."

"Sure wish there was something we could do," Earl chimed in. "Warrender, right? Was that his name too?"

"I was only married once, and not for long."

"Why come here, of all places? Any clue?"

"Seems like he'd a pile of debt. But as much as Roy'd get into trouble, he'd always find some way out. I'm not convinced he's dead."

The track, hard-packed, ran a little way as it wove between tree trunks, then climbed as it entered the cave, hugging the inside wall. Earl and Virginia hung back to let Annette precede them. A strange euphoria came over her, perhaps from sharing her concern with sympathetic people right at the spot where Roy was last known to be.

The dirty white of the limestone seemed to suck to itself what light there was. She could barely see and felt as though she'd entered some vast cathedral and was perched like a bird on a shelf halfway to the roof. The dark shapes of bats and who knew what else circled eerily. From down below came the disorienting thunder of water, and a thudding boom like a cannon.

Stalactites hung in groups like cow's udders. She'd read how they dripped virgin water that the ancient Mayans collected and used in ceremonies. A marketable resource perhaps that somehow Roy was onto. In none of what she'd read could she divine a reason for his being here. No tales of buried treasure, no hidden mineral deposits.

Was there tourist potential? A tropical Carlsbad Caverns crying out to be transformed into a luxury resort with all the trappings: riding, canoeing, hiking, golf, expeditions to nearby ruins. *Kjelborg & McKenzie*. Was that it?

Or a mythological pageant: the legendary journey of the Hero Twins and their trials in the House of Darkness—in *son et lumière*—along with burning incense to honor ancestors, and the sacrifice of birds, dogs and children to the gods? Massed choirs along the far side of the abyss, perhaps? She called a long drawn out, "Ro-o-o-y," which lost itself in replication. And heard the echo of a different sound, repeated, deep and urgent, from where, and what, she couldn't exactly say.

Annette turned, the others had done the same. Behind them, someone was running. Against the light, she could see only that it was a man and he was waving his arms. "Lady, lady, thanks to God you are safe," Ascensión panted. "I forget to waan you." He walked on ahead, examining the narrow path, then stopped and beckoned.

Annette saw a slight discoloration in the rock, the size of a tin tray. A closer look revealed an indentation, maybe a few inches deep. Carefully sidestepping it and looking from the other side, as directed, she saw that a hole angled clean through the ledge they were standing on, forming a chute wide enough to fit a man. Through it, far below, glimmered a ribbon of foam. It wasn't just her own narrow escape she was thinking of.

A somewhat shaken group filed out of the cave that morning. Ascensión looked wonderingly at Annette and shook his head as if some other-worldly power must surely protect her. "I stretching out for my faaty winks, eyes close y'know, then it come to me jus' like dat." He flicked his fingers. "Las' year I've a customer, American, he pretty near faal in. Jus' like you aalmos' faal in." He patted the trunk of a giant tree growing at the mouth of the cave, its roots arching like buttresses he could have walked under. "Ceiba, lucky tree of my people." Dislodging a thumb size black object, one of many stuck to the gray spiky bark, he held it out to her.

"What are they?"

"Cicadas climb out an' leave their skins." Like Roy, she thought. A dried-out husk sticking to the bark of my imagination. Maybe he did plunge to his death down there. Or maybe not. Did it really matter any more? Her hand instinctively closed over the carapace and crushed it, and she began to sob.

The pressure of an arm at her waist, guiding her, felt good. "Take a deep breath, dearie, and don't you worry about a thing, you hear me?"

On the way back they stopped by the forest station because Ascensión thought there was a clinic there. After driving around and beeping they managed to raise an old man. Clinic closed today, he said. Earl decided he'd leave off some toothbrushes and snake bite kits anyway. He hopped out and knocked at the man's door.

"He serve you a beer or something?" Virginia asked tartly when, some minutes later, her brother reappeared.

He winked. "Just an ice-cold coke."

Down the road a truckload of stripped-to-the-waist British Tommies overtook them. Virginia declared them the cutest thing she'd seen in a coon's age. Earl said they looked like something out of a can. They were, Annette agreed, a quite extraordinary pink.

"Dey from de training camp on the plateau," Ascensión gestured, and went to great lengths to show Annette a rare wild orchid in an effort to cheer her up. They ate their sandwiches on a bluff overlooking a waterfall.

Lying in the shade, watching falcons breasting the thermal air current above the falls, its depths hidden in a mist of spray, Annette tried to come to terms with herself. What did she want? Was it Roy, or was it just that he stood for the nearest thing she'd had to a normal happy life? Or was it Colin, whole instead of in increasingly infrequent bits? Turning onto her stomach, she buried her face in her arms.

Earl and Virginia, a little way off, exchanged glances.

FAX SIX

Send to: SURGE, LONDON
Sender: IN VESTIGIUM, INC., NEW YORK

September 5th

As anticipated, the mystery surrounding the Obs's activities is at last unraveling, as the waiting game played by the watchers begins to pay off.

Yesterday's excursion to the mountain caves proved enlightening. The Obs shared with the watchers her obsession with finding her long since divorced husband, Roy Warrender, a Canadian entrepreneur who vanished over the summer with substantial debts. Her visit to San Ignacio was occasioned by his supposedly having spent time in the area. A rental car, linked to him, was found abandoned near one of the caves. The Obs, exploring the cave with our watchers, was only saved from a fall by a timely warning from the driver/guide.

One puzzling question concerns Ottawa Man. The same driver/guide identified him from our photo as having been his passenger to the caves the previous year. This ties in time-wise with his name in the Visitor Book at the Mayan ruins. Less credibly, an old man at a forest station said he could have been a gringo he saw in the area at roughly the time Warrender disappeared. Though any white man might pass for him, and British soldiers patrol there to guard against hostile incursions from Guatemala.

This morning the Obs informed the watchers that she had received a call from the Toronto Police Missing Persons Department. Warrender—or someone answering his description—was reported to be in the extreme south of the country. She was clearly excited and has an appointment the day after tomorrow in Punta Gorda, the southern district headquarters, with someone from the Belize Special Branch. She has accepted the watchers' offer of a ride from San Ignacio to Belize City tomorrow morning for her flight south to Punta Gorda.

In light of the above, do you wish your instruction of yesterday to stand, viz. that in an emergency we prioritize protection of the Obs even at the risk of detection?

CHAPTER EIGHTEEN

In Punta Gorda, Belize, at a little after five on a Sunday morning, Annette is sitting on steps leading to the back verandah of the District Health Centre staring out to where the sea should be. The night is pitch black, with just the buzz of a fisherman's boat heading out to his nets breaking the stillness. The ocean—here the Gulf of Honduras—gradually begins to reveal itself and she distinguishes the blacker shape of a cloud that takes up half the sky. Behind this behemoth a contrasting lightening is almost imperceptibly beginning, and under it a pale, thin strip appears dividing sea from sky. Fascinated, she observes the dark mass slowly breaking into two halves which the sun, rising, backlights with a flaming fire in which they seem to squirm and writhe.

Annette, in jeans, sneakers and a headscarf, has managed to shrink her impedimenta to fit a small shoulder bag that sits next to her. She was told to be ready at five, but so far only herself and a young CARE bee expert have shown up. By six everyone has trickled in: the district health officer, a couple of health educators, a Mennonite nurse, a government dentist, three women returning to their village and, finally, with a bad case of early morning blues, Special Branch officer Elvis P. Ruiz.

At last a throaty rumble announces their boat, and everyone clambers aboard. The captain—a vast and jovial Garifuna man with CONCH KING embroidered on his cap—is eager to be off. Soon they are ploughing southward along the coast on a smooth sea.

"Suppose we find him?" Annette asks Ruiz. She is propped against her bag in the prow. Ruiz, wedged in by boxes and paraphernalia, is facing her. The white of his outfit gleams through a transparent rain slicker. He does not look happy and pretends—through the noise of the engine—not to hear her question. The previous evening, in a more communicative mood, he explained developments. A Peace Corps worker—an agricultural expert on a tour of the area they were bound for—had seen a man, an American he supposed, living in one of the remote villages. He'd seemed disoriented, not sure what country he was in or where he was from. He knew neither Spanish nor Kekchi, the local tongue, wouldn't give his name, and professed to be searching for a lost archeological site. When he mentioned this strange encounter to friends, they recalled a piece in the paper about a missing Canadian, and alerted the police. Toronto, in turn, was informed and Missing Persons there requested an on the spot investigation. In Belize City it was front page news. Ruiz had brought the latest editions.

The prospect of nursing Roy back to health and happiness thrills Annette, though Detective sergeant MacFaddin, on the phone, sounded a good deal less sanguine. Gazing from the boat at the jagged line of the Maya Mountains, she wonders where they could go. Perhaps the Florida Keys or the Bahamas, somewhere to be alone together and get reacquainted. His debts? Surely something could be worked out. Dolphins, shimmering as they break the surface, reflect her mood. Rain clouds, scarcely noticed, gather like a low-slung ceiling in the distance.

An hour out of Punta Gorda, as Captain Conch maneuvers into the estuary of the Sarstoon River—Belize's southern border with Guatemala—the first drops fall. Annette hunches cross-legged under her umbrella, her bag in her lap, watching water fill the bottom of the boat. A smell of death announces the bloated body of a horse, long before—legs outstretched—it floats by. After the rain there's still an hour to go up this smooth, wide river and one of its tributaries. The bee expert points out three different woodpeckers, cormorants, blue herons, greater blue herons, greater egrets. White spider irises line the banks, where mangroves give way to towering ceibas. A brown rifle-toting arm waves them to a hidden landing where two Mayans wait with a packhorse.

A long slog down a jungle path, where powder blue butterflies the size of handkerchiefs drift ambiguously, brings them to a group of thatched dwellings set amid a circle of forested hills. On its concrete plinth, waiting to be grandly opened, sits the zinc-roofed health centre. "It's not here where he was sighted, it's the next place," remarks Ruiz.

Annette suspects that he blames her for their coming, that it's a man's right to disappear if he wants to. The prospect of seeing Roy has sustained her thus far. She's not sure how much further she has left in her. A crowd of men and boys watch them as they cool their faces and wash the mud from their shoes at a little stream. There are no women in sight.

"These people," says Ruiz, "they come across the border. They haven't lived here long. They are very afraid. If they knew I was Special Branch they'd run and hide."

Suddenly, from all points, brightly dressed women and girls converge. The ceremony is about to begin.

Some five hours later Annette is approaching the next village. She is muddy all the way up one side, her sneakers squish at every step and her jeans are steaming wet from wading through streams. Her tongue, despite frequent gulps from her water bottle, is parched. One hand is swollen from a thorny tree she grabbed to steady herself. Her head is filled with Ruiz's description of scorpions, snakes, evil spirits, jaguars: all the things that can jump out at a person in the jungle. She has long since lost sight of the Mennonite nurse who skipped along in a skirt and blouse almost as deftly as the Mayans themselves. Ruiz has stayed with her only because, she suspects, he'd have a lot of explaining to do if he lost her. Now and then he curses his horse as it slips and slithers under him.

Annette balked at riding after the wily beast first scraped her off against a tree, then lay down on top of her in the mud. She hardly cares if she never sees Roy again, and certainly won't visit him in prison, which is where he belongs if only for dragging her through hell and gone. Besides, what would the Roy she knew be doing in a place like this? The Roy she knew? Why go on fooling herself? Sometimes it takes profound physical exhaustion for mental clarity to break through.

She drags herself to a tap connected to a water tank and drinks deeply. Someone yells at her not to wash in drinking water. On the verge of tears, she slinks off after Ruiz towards a stream. His white outfit is now piebald. "People still at work in the fields," he says, "harvesting the rice."

"So where's Roy?" The idea of him toiling in some hot and swampy patch of rice almost makes her laugh. "Do you really think he's here?"

Ruiz unhitches his revolver and lays it carefully on a rock. Between them they turn the stream brown with their scrubbing. "Leave him to me. Everything's cool. Plan already taking shape in my head. You'll see."

As soon as he leaves, she changes into her swimsuit and cools off in a shallow pool among the rocks. As the aches and pains of the last hours slowly soak away, she starts to feel better and kicks her legs wildly in relief; and as the splashing ends, thinks she hears laughter. Kicking again—was it an echo?—this time she hears screams. On a rocky ledge behind her sit a bunch of four or five year olds having the time of their life, at her expense.

"Well, hi there! Good evening," she calls out.

All together, "Good morning!" they yell.

"How are you?"

"Fine, thank you!" Annette is surprised. No one in the last village seemed to know English.

Nudging each other, giggling and squirming, after several false starts they launch into song. It's a moment or two before Annette catches on. No, surely. *Yellow Submarine?*

"That's very nice," she tells them. "Where did you learn that?" But they hide their faces and she slips into her spare pair of jeans. Roy? She walks back up the hill. When villagers trickle in from the fields, he is not among them.

It's the middle of the night. Annette is stretched out on a hammock that is tied to the cross beams of what seems like a large barn, but is actually someone's house. The gentle snoring at her feet is from the hammock of the Mennonite nurse. Beyond her, in a third hammock, is one of the Mayan health educators. Up the far end is the family of their host, the local community health worker. The walls are of loosely spaced wooden planks affording a slight but welcome breeze through the cracks. It's a moonlit night and she is aware of the gentle movement of the trees outside. Reaching for her shoulder bag on a nail on the wall she fumbles for the flashlight and checks the time on her watch.

She's lain in this hammock now for six hours. After dusk came dinner with the family, a thin hot gruel with chunks of chicken and tortillas. Then it was bedtime and she'd fallen into a tired sleep.

Somewhere beneath her a dog growls and a hen ruffles its feathers in the dust. From outside comes the soft thud thudding on packed earth of an approaching animal, quite close now, and the nostrilly exhalation of a horse, its dark shape passing just a few feet from her head, its sweet hairy smell wafting like a ghost through the room. The figure leading the horse seems vaguely familiar. Sometimes you see things you really only imagine, or imagine later you've seen things that weren't there at all. The footsteps die away in the night.

The next thing she knows, the fire at the far end of the room is being stoked and women are pounding corn. It's four o'clock. At five the Voice of America news in English crackles to life. "An earthquake has flattened large areas of ..." Surely on some other planet. A few hours later, Annette is sheltering from a heavy drizzle under the overhanging thatch of a hut, watching as sparring cock turkeys are separated by two tiny girls who drag one off by a wing. Her mood matches the dripping, smoke-infused sadness of the weather. She can't help but think of a certain slatted barn in far-off Connecticut.

At the feast in honor of the health center, Annette feels awkward and isolated. They sit on low benches around an open fire on which a big pot of *puch*—cornmeal dumplings wrapped in cohune palm leaves—is keeping warm. A woman does the rounds with a plastic bucket of cocoa. As Annette dips a calabash into the grey, cool, bitter liquid and drinks, such a look she gets—of pity, wonder, incomprehension—that she almost chokes.

"I tell 'em this is last chance to surrender the gringo," Ruiz whispers to her. "I know they hiding him somewhere, out in the fields maybe. I tell 'em I come back with a helicopter, shoot up the whole place. That's the language they understand, these *Guatemaltecos*."

"What did you say about me?"

"You come all the way from the States to find him, his wife, the mother of his children." She was glad not to have shared with him her vision in the night.

A further three-hour hike brings what remains of the party to a settlement on the banks of the Temash, where the Mennonite nurse is stationed and Captain Conch is waiting impatiently in the boat to ferry them home. Poor Ruiz. He is the last to stagger in, literally and figuratively browned off.

The Temash is, if anything, more winding than the Sarstoon. As twilight sets in, a blue heron glides ahead of them from tree to tall tree, a guiding spirit, but darkness falls before they reach the sea. Out in the gulf the boat hits a submerged log at speed and rears out of the water. No damage is done, save to nerves frayed to numbness, and they ride the moon path northeast in silence past the blinking, oddly reassuring pylons of a VOA transmitting station.

Back in Punta Gorda, at the hotel, ready to crawl into bed, Annette discovers that her wallet is missing. A cruel end to a day when just about all hope seemed extinguished.

FAX SEVEN

Send to: SURGE, LONDON
Sender: IN VESTIGIUM, INC., NEW YORK

September 7th

After dropping the Obs at the airport on Thursday morning, the watchers continued to Punta Gorda, arriving on Sunday to discover that the Obs had left early by boat, catching a ride with a party of health officials visiting the area where Warrender had been reported. Accompanying her was a detective from police headquarters in Belize City.

She arrived back in Punta Gorda on Monday evening, and went straight to her room at the hotel. To add to the general air of perplexity, a familiar figure turned up Sunday evening at a restaurant where the watchers were eating dinner: Ottawa Man. He ate alone at the bar, and drank considerably. A watcher followed him to his hotel, the only reasonable one in town, where the Obs is also staying. At the front desk he reportedly asked when she'd be back, and was told Monday. He is registered under the name Tom Barton.

CHAPTER NINETEEN

Annette slept as she'd never slept before. It was after ten when she opened her eyes and nearer eleven when she managed to coax her aching body into a shower. Only then, with the familiar fragrance of her shampoo billowing steamily around her, did she recall the lost wallet. "Damn!" she cried, loud enough for the maid, who'd put a head round the door hoping to make up the room, to snatch it back. The wallet contained her credit card and charge cards, about a hundred dollars U.S. and her driver license. She'd hidden travelers' checks and a few bucks in the suitcase left at the hotel, so she wasn't penniless.

How did it happen? The wallet was in the zippered inside pocket of her bag which hadn't been out of her sight the whole trip. Needing no money, she'd not missed it. Wet from the shower she feverishly searched again—her bag, the suitcase, the closet. "Damn, damn, damn." It was then that she saw the envelope lying on the floor by the door. ANNETTE, it said. Ripping it open, her mind still on the cards and the bother of cancelling them and what on earth good a Lord & Taylor charge was going to be to anyone in the jungle, she read: *We have to talk—away from all the others. I'm across the bay on the Guatemala side, in Puerto Barrios. Hotel del Norte. You can't miss it as you get off the ferry which leaves Punta Gorda at 2. Ticket enclosed. Get an exit stamp in your passport at the police station by the dock before boarding. I love you and need you.*

It was unsigned. It didn't have to be. Poised in the middle of the room, naked and still as an artist's model, her thoughts—a minute ago careening out of control—were instantly lassoed. *I love you and need you.* The main thing was not to let Ruiz know, or for that matter Earl and Virginia, who might insist on escorting her.

After changing some money, she joined them for lunch at a Chinese place they'd 'discovered'. Apparently Ruiz had already filled them in on their jungle adventure—with himself in the hero's role. Annette, pleading exhaustion, bowed out of a visit to a clinic. As soon as they drove off, she packed a fresh bag and told the desk she'd be gone overnight.

Now it was after five. In the sober end-of-day light, as the ferry churned landward, Annette took in the wide curve of a gentle bay with its mangroves and colorful shacks on stilts spilling into the water. "That's it, see, blue with white trim, the Hotel del Norte." Annette saw a sturdy old dame of a building on the shorefront. "And there's the train station." She'd fallen in with an enthusiastic young American returning to language school in Guatemala City. "Sit on the porch at twilight and sense the cotton flounces and high starched collars moving across it when the train from Guaté steams in, and the lithe Garifuna boys shouldering the luggage. Those were the days."

Straining her eyes, Annette imagined movement on that porch, the pacing figure of a man. Or perhaps he was sitting quietly, watching their approach. Would he come down to meet her?

The formalities over, she walked to the hotel and climbed its wooden steps on aching legs. A couple of rattan rockers faced each other in a corner, and as Annette's hopeful eyes passed over them, one seemed to nod sagely to its companion. Pushing through a door into a dark interior of mirrors and polished wood, she glanced quickly about her. At the bar, a thickset stranger in a tan suit leaned over a drink. At a corner table a woman nursed a baby. An elderly man, polishing a glass, looked up inquiringly. "*Me encuentro con alguien aqui,*" she said in her best high school Spanish.

"I'm sure he won't detain you, Madame," the man responded in perfect English. "Meanwhile, may I fetch you something?"

"Long and non-alcoholic would hit the nail on the head. And is there—?"

He gestured. I must look a fright, she thought. Touching up her face, she wondered in what ways it differed from the one she'd looked at so despairingly all those years ago in the tiny yellow bathroom on East 88th Street the morning after Roy walked out. *I love you and need you.* But who did he love and need? Had he made allowances for a tougher woman—applying eyeliner—who, while not utterly disillusioned, had come to terms with life's realities.

On the bar was a fresh drink. "I'll manage," she said, taking the glass from the tray and stepping out into the twilight. A figure rose up from one of the rockers. "You may need something stronger than that," he remarked casually.

To forestall whatever it was he had in mind—a handshake, a hug, a peck on the cheek—Annette made straight for the other chair. "Where's Roy?" she said in a flat voice.

"Aha." Kjelborg subsided. "I was afraid you might ask."

"Well? What are you two up to exactly?"

Kjelborg eased a hand around the inside of his open collar. It seemed to Annette he was wearing the same outfit she'd last seen him in at the Russian restaurant on Madison Avenue. "You make us sound like a couple of schoolboy pranksters," he said. "I'm afraid it's much worse than that."

"I'd like to speak to Roy." She was surprised at the tone of her voice.

Kjelborg sadly shook his head. *"No es posible."*

"What do you mean?" She held out Roy's note.

Kjelborg took it, folded the page in half and, using a notebook for support, wrote something on the back. She glanced at it, got up and went to where light was spilling out from the bar. The writing on both sides of the paper, word for word, was Roy's. Moving to the edge of the porch, she stared unseeing into the gloom. Behind her the barman was asking if anything further was required.

"Same again," Kjelborg ordered. "And a beer for the lady."

Annette returned to her chair and sat down. "So why am I here?" she asked bleakly.

"Because we need to talk—the two of us—and this seemed a convenient place. If you'd only listened back in New York, you'd have saved yourself a lot of trouble."

"Listened! You walked out on me."

"With good reason. We were under observation. By the same crowd that 'borrowed' my wallet, no doubt."

"Where is he?"

Kjelborg slumped back in his chair and addressed the ceiling. "Lord, what a jerk I've been." He sat up. "I'd no idea you were that gone on him, Annette. I still don't understand. You looked smart, successful. I couldn't conceive of your caring that much about a guy who treated you the way he did, whom you hadn't set eyes on in twenty years."

"Kjelborg," she said, exasperation getting the upper hand, "just tell me the truth for once. Now."

"Roy's dead. That's it, I've said it. D E A D."

The ensuing silence was prolonged by the barman's arrival with the drinks. As he padded off over the floorboards, Annette whispered, "You mean in the last day or two? Tell me."

"Weeks ago."

"But I thought I saw him the night before last. I guess not."

If Kjelborg was surprised, he didn't show it. "Go on," he invited, "tell me more." She explained about her night in the hammock. "Well of course," he sneered. "Weren't the papers full of it—the mysterious gringo, showing up in some village or other in the back of beyond. How do you think I knew where to find you? It's a recognized psychological phenomenon. Accounts for half the world's ghost stories, and all our divine visitations. That wasn't Roy, you saw, poor bastard. I wish to God it had been."

"How can you be so sure?"

"Because," he looked her in the eye, "I saw him die." It wasn't till Kjelborg whipped the red silk handkerchief from his jacket pocket and thrust it at her that Annette realized she was crying. Ignoring the offer, she rummaged in her bag for a Kleenex. "It's not a pretty story. I'd give a hell of a lot not to tell it. But frankly, Annette, you've forced my hand."

Spare us the handwringing, she thought.

"*Kjelborg & McKenzie*, remember? That's where you came in. Thanks to some precocious, Gorgonzola-guzzling feline, for chrissakes. Well, I admit, you only heard half the story. Yes, I got Roy out of Canada, out of the clutches of his creditors. Yes, I got him on that south-bound banana boat. Yes, he said he had a sure fire way to recoup his millions. What he didn't have was seed money, enough to prime the pump, and, fool that I am, I loaned it to him, just about every cent I had.

"On paper, it looked feasible. Basically turning a vast underground system of caverns into the world's largest toxic waste dump. Unpopulated, government-owned land. All you needed for backers to line up at your door was the permit. And the permit process—according to Roy—was a synch. That's where my savings came in."

"I imagined it was some sort of crazy venture he'd dreamed up," murmured Annette.

"From Scientists Cliffs—I'm sure I told you this bit—I drove Roy's car to Dulles International, where I left it. We'd arranged to meet again in Belize at the inn in San Ignacio, where Roy, aka Calvin Mackenzie, would be staying. On the appointed day I flew to Belize City and took a bus upcountry. Together we went to inspect the caves. Roy had sworn they were granite, leak proof. The first one we entered—I'm no expert, but it was obvious—was limestone. Porous like a sieve. I stopped to scrape the wall with my knife as Roy charged ahead. A minute or two later I heard the most blood-curdling scream, like those howler monkeys they have down here, and at first I thought it was one. I ran to help him, and if it hadn't been for the flashlight Roy must have dropped, being on, I'd have gone in myself. A bloody great booby trap right in the middle of the path."

"I know, I saw it."

"Ah, went up for a look, did you? Then you know what I'm talking about. Believe me, there's no way anyone could have survived that fall. I scrambled around for hours searching, calling, listening, nothing, Roy had vanished."

"Why did you go away and leave the car? Why didn't you go for help?" Annette practically shouted at him.

"I'll tell you why," he said, "only don't judge me." He waited till he saw she was calmer. "I thought I was doing him a favor. I still think so. Annette, Annette, don't hate me for what I'm going to tell you." He leaned towards her. "Roy killed Kristi Aranda."

"I don't believe you. How could he? Why?"

"He told me. And he told me how."

Annette closed her eyes and sank back in her chair. When she opened them, the barman was hovering nearby. Kjelborg called for brandies.

"It was a perfect end for Roy," he went on. "The end of running away. I walked back to the trail and hitched a ride with a bunch of Tommies as far as the main road, then a bus to Belize City and a flight home. I figured they'd find the car. He'd checked out of the inn and his stuff was in it. The body would wash downstream sooner or later, be identified, and the whole affair would be closed. Then along you come, scrabbling up the past. You've no idea how you've complicated my life, Annette."

"I guess not," she said wearily. "I'm sorry. My brain isn't functioning. I just need time for a good think."

"They do a passable fish dinner here. I owe you. Barracuda?"

"Thanks," she looked vacantly at her bag on the floor. "I think I'll just go to bed."

Annette's head was full of questions, questions that wouldn't let her sleep. Round and round they went, faster and faster. Ring-a-ring-a-roses, we all fall down. But they didn't. Kjelborg's tale sickened her. The tale, and how he told it. The night was muggy, the pillow damp from sweat and tears. A mosquito wouldn't leave her alone. At last she got up and stepped onto the upstairs porch and stood facing the bay, aware of unidentifiable night noises.

Cack-cack-cack-cack, somewhere out there a strange bird sounded.

A sharp click behind her made her start: Kjelborg, in a silk dressing gown, his hair ruffled. "I saw you standing there and thought, how sensible," he murmured, coming alongside.

"I couldn't sleep. I felt like I'd sprung a leak and everything was draining out of me."

"I take it, in my shoes, you'd have done differently," he prompted gently.

"No, no. I mean, well, perhaps. I'd not have had your presence of mind."

"But—?"

"That's it. I don't want you to think—" She forced herself to look at him. "Well, there were a couple of things."

"Fire away. You may not get another crack." Her look of alarm seemed to amuse him.

"You figured Roy would turn up downstream somewhere and be identified and that would be that. Well it's been a month, and according to the police no ID was found in the car. It was only when I was with Special Branch in Belize City the day I arrived and a receipt from the San Ignacio Inn fell out of a map, that they had a name, Calvin McKenzie. Up to then there was nothing to link a missing Canadian businessman with Roy."

"If there was no ID in the car, Roy must have had some on him when he fell. He had a passport in his own name presumably."

"But where's the body?"

"Annette, Annette, my little lamb, my innocent. What's happening to us all?" Reluctantly, she let him hold her, wishing it was Roy. "We know not what we do."

She looked up, puzzled, and was surprised to see he was crying. Her fingers found his arm and she returned its comforting pressure. What a little moonlight can do.

FAX EIGHT

Send to: SURGE, LONDON

Sender: IN VESTIGIUM, INC., NEW YORK

September 8th

At lunch with the watchers, the Obs seemed reluctant to discuss the expedition to the jungle villages. She returned to her room ostensibly to rest. The watchers later learned from the front desk that she would be away overnight.

From the Special Branch officer who accompanied the Obs to the jungle, the watchers were able to corroborate that she is indeed in cahoots with the Homicide and Missing Persons Division of the Toronto police, assisting in the search for her late husband.

Detective Ruiz also revealed that the Obs received an exit stamp in her passport at the police station shortly before boarding a ferry for the 3 to 4 hour trip across the bay to Puerto Barrios, Guatemala. Also elicited was the fact that Ottawa Man, aka Tom Barton, aka Soren Gustavus Kjelborg had himself left for Puerto Barrios the previous day in a hired boat.

There being no watchers in Puerto Barrios at this time, we are taking steps to remedy this expeditiously, and will be back in touch as soon as we are in a position to ascertain what the Obs is doing over there.

CHAPTER TWENTY

"What will you do now?" Asked Kjelborg in the morning.

Annette stared at the brown filter tip of a cigarette rolling back and forth in the breeze across the planking of the porch. A bit the way she felt. Finally she said, "Go home. Get on with what's left of my life." They had carried their breakfast coffees out from the dining room. The day was not yet hot. "Trouble is, it's *not* home, not any more. That's one thing that's come out of all this. Thanks, Roy." She smiled.

Kjelborg flashed her a glance from under the thatch of his eyebrows. "So what cooling streams does the old hart pant for?"

"Who knows? Something will turn up." They listened to the day unfolding around them. "And you?"

"Me? Smite the sounding furrows, one presumes. Seek a newer world, and all that."

"Why," Annette appealed, more to herself than to her companion, "why, why would he do a thing like that? It makes no sense." She turned to Kjelborg. "Will we ever know, do you think?"

"I doubt he knew himself. He was horrified. I think that's the word. He told himself so many fibs, did Roy, over the years. And when they began to trip him up, the easiest thing was just to believe them. He thought he was in love, I suppose. Vane, self-deluding love. Probably she laughed at him, pitied his obsession. As simple as that. Laughter, in that sort of context, can be devastating."

"It's not as if he was some kind of raging beast. He hated football."

"Twenty years is a long time. Appetites, they develop, they grow. The lion that tastes human flesh comes back for more."

"Kjelborg!"

"Status—let's face it, that's what Roy craved, and he found a way to get it. He snared you, Annette. He outgrew you. He snared Selina. He outgrew Selina. Imagine: ahead on the plains rise the glittering towers of Castle Haggard. Lance in hand, Sir Roy, on frothing steed, approaches its gates. The drawbridge is lowered. He clatters across. But try as he may, there's an inner sanctum he can never penetrate, unless— He's pulled it off before, why not now?"

"Oh, please."

"My dear?"

"Tell me what Roy told you."

Kjelborg leaned back, stretching his legs. "It was her utter indifference that infuriated him, her look as she turned away. It must have been brutally obvious she'd no more feelings for him than for a beggar in the street. He caught her from behind and—"

"No."

He smirked, "You wish to be spared the details?"

"So all these years you've known."

"What would you have done?"

"But the family, imagine what they've been through. Shouldn't I go to them, at least put their minds at rest. God, in some weird way, I feel responsible."

"By all means, go to them. And when they slam the door in your face, shout it through the mail slot. Roy did it! Hey everyone, it was Roy!" He smiled. "They don't want to know, Annette. Just as Selina didn't want to know. It's over. They're only going to hate you. Of course, that's maybe what you want."

"You're probably right," she conceded. "The police thought so too."

"Oh, and you'll go to Homicide, to your precious detective. Headlines in all the Toronto papers"—he cupped his hands —"KILLER NAMED IN SOCIETY SEX SLAYING!" And dropping his voice, "Roy's gone, Kristi's gone. Think of the living, Annette. Think of his son, if you like."

She nodded numbly. "That detective in Toronto, she said it wasn't him. His hands"—she flexed her fingers—"not a strangler's hands, she said, not the strength."

"If I were you," said Kjelborg, glancing involuntarily at his own paws, "I'd let lying dogs sleep, to coin a phrase. But please yourself." He stood up. "If you'll excuse me I'll go and drum up some transport to return you to Punta Gorda, assuming that's where you want to go."

"Thanks, I'll just take the ferry."

"You'll have to wait till Friday. Two a week."

She watched him loping down towards the waterfront, till the street swallowed him up. Strange man, she thought, recollecting their night encounter. He'd picked his moment. She was never more vulnerable. Yet something of himself had been disclosed, the bluster in him lifting briefly like a mist to reveal a lake of sadness, where someone perhaps had drowned. Why was he here? What was he up to? She hadn't got around to asking.

The mainland was a faint mound of hills. Guatemala? Honduras? Annette didn't know. To the east the sun laid a cloak of blinding gold over the open sea. Turning, she thought she could just see the jagged ridge of the Maya Mountains heaving into view. She was the sole passenger on the fast launch that Kjelborg had conjured up and—incredibly—paid for. The boatman, a grimy Guatemalteco, spoke no English or much of anything, but chewed constantly on a toothpick and refused to meet her eye. Apart from a flotilla of pelicans flying low across their wake, an ant of a freighter on the eastern horizon and the dot of another boat against the receding hills, they had the world to themselves.

Not that Annette would have paid much attention had they been in the midst of a regatta. She was alone in a stew of her own thoughts, the more so for the breeze rushing against her face and flapping the ends of her headscarf. Either she was speeding head-long into an unknown future or in full retreat from a past that had spun itself out. Time would decide. Every so often a sheaf of spray, hitting her broadside, brought to mind the immediate present.

Happening to gaze about after a particularly drenching shower caught her dozing, she was at first mystified, then alarmed, to see no sign of land. Not a bump or protrusion any-where. The sun was now high overhead. By her watch they were almost two hours out of Puerto Barrios, and at the rate they were going—surely more than twice the speed of the ferry—should by now have reached Punta Gorda. Where were the Maya Moun-tains, a landmark they'd been heading towards rising across the bay? The one comfort was the sight of another boat some few hundred yards behind them. She watched as it appeared and reappeared over the boatman's shoulder, and noticed how un-easily aware of it he seemed to be, almost as if they were in a race. The boat stayed in their wake, neither gaining nor losing ground. Annette made out three or four people on board. Clambering back to where the boatman sat with one arm loosely draped over the tiller, she pointed to her right. "Belize?" She yelled. "Punta Gorda?"

"*Si si*," he brushed her off with an impatient nod and she crawled back.

No doubt about it, all was not well. She could smell it, breathe it, taste it in the salty spray. Pirates, perhaps? Confirming her worst fears, the boatman fumbled under his seat and, from a lump of dirty rags, pulled out a gun. With the barest glance at his passenger, he cocked it and placed it in his lap, then cut the power to a trickle, the boat, slowing suddenly, rocking back on itself. The second boat, instead of following in their wake, turned slightly in a flanking movement. Predator-like, Annette thought, getting set for the kill.

Slowly, suspiciously, the two boats closed on each other, till only some hundred yards separated them, and the rough hand of the boatman tightened around his revolver. In the other boat, they were crouching low against the gunwale. At last she was able to read the name on its prow, CONCH KING. From what she could see of the man at the tiller, he was large and black and the cap on his head looked familiar.

"*Policia, policia...*" the words came rolling over the water. Other words followed, Spanish words that were lost on Annette. Her boatman left the tiller and knelt on the baseboard, weapon in hand. She tried to scream, He's armed, he's got a gun!—something, anything to warn them—but all she did was gag. Then came the crackle of shots. She felt herself grabbed from behind and something press against her head.

In the other boat, Ruiz—she saw him clearly—was standing in a firing position, arms stiff out in front of him, aiming, for all she knew, at her. He was bawling something in Spanish and the boats now were so close Annette could hear every word and prayed the boatman could too. He smelled of smoke and grease and sweat that held the tang of fear, and as they drifted in a ghastly pirouette, so he turned Annette. Ruiz kept talking, talking the boats closer and closer. She could see Earl now, and he too seemed to be armed, and behind him Virginia.

At last the boats were bobbing side by side in the swell and Captain Conch with a boathook was drawing them together. At the point where they touched stood Virginia, arms outstretched. "Very slowly move towards Virginia," Ruiz instructed, not taking his eyes off the boatman. "Take your time."

Annette sensed the man's weapon still on her as she climbed into Virginia's embrace and froze, slowly letting out her breath. "Y'all just relax now. Everything gonna be fine." Behind her she heard Ruiz and the boatman in heated discussion and the word *gas* repeated.

"I'm going to turn around," Annette whispered, doing so in time to see the boatman's gun disappear into the green depths. A moment later, with the crunch of metal on tarp, a gas can landed in his boat. Captain Conch adjusted the throttle and Conch King veered away.

"Shoulda finished him off," Ruiz spat out, staring at the diminishing vessel.

"Be my guest." Earl tossed his own weapon to him. It bounced feebly on the boards, a plastic water bottle.

"My bag!" Annette cried.

"Doan worry," said the captain, "someone pick it up before long. Dat fella not goin' far on what I give him. Jus' what he ask for: de can."

When she'd calmed down sufficiently, Annette asked how they happened to be so conveniently at hand.

"Why, we were out fishin'," said Virginia.

"No, really."

"It was Elvis Presley," she sent him a little finger wave, "when he found out where you'd got to. We kind of invited ourselves along. Took a bit of persuadin', but it all worked out for the best in the end."

"I'll say. What on earth was he up to, that man, do you think?"

"S'pect I could guess. Robbin' you blind, maybe rapin' you, and feedin' you to a passing shark."

By the time the Maya Mountains began inching over the horizon, the drone of the engine was about the only sound heard aboard the Conch King, her passengers yielding to the languor of a tropical afternoon. "Phew! Some trip," yawned Virginia.

Annette agreed, thinking in rather broader terms. Was it only a month ago she'd picked up the phone in her apartment and thought it was Roy on the line? Seemed like years.

FAX NINE

Send to: SURGE, LONDON
Sender: IN VESTIGIUM, INC., NEW YORK

September 9th

Early this morning the watchers in Punta Gorda were informed by Detective Ruiz of the Belize police that, in communication with his office and with the Toronto police, he had commandeered a fast boat to take him across the bay to Puerto Barrios, Guatemala, to check on the Obs's activities and report back. The watchers persuaded him to let them go along.

Hardly had they arrived in Puerto Barrios than the Obs and Ottawa Man were sighted walking along the quay. They embraced, she climbed into a motorboat—the sole passenger—and he waved her off. To the watchers' party, following at a distance, it soon became clear that—far from returning to Belize—they were headed for the open sea.

Had the boat not slowed—apparently for lack of fuel—there's no knowing what might have happened. After a tense stand-off, the Obs transferred to the watchers' boat which returned her safely to Punta Gorda. The boatman was subsequently apprehended. Further details will be forthcoming as they become available.

What is Ottawa Man's relationship with the Obs? Why the meeting in Puerto Barrios when he'd turned up in Punta Gorda just the day before? Why not wait and meet her there? These are among the questions we continue to probe. Since her return from the jungle the Obs has seemed preoccupied and has not shared with the watchers what is on her mind, as earlier at the cave.

She flies to Belize City tomorrow morning.

CHAPTER TWENTY ONE

Annette, back in New York, found a message from Detective sergeant MacFaddin on the answering machine: please call when you get in. That was all. Ominously, nothing from Colin; her note lay untouched. The apartment felt sucked of air. For a moment she stood still, then—rousing herself—undressed and jumped in the shower.

If she spoke to MacFaddin she'd have to tell her about Roy. Sooner or later, no doubt, it would all come out, but with no help from her. Roy the lover, Roy the embezzler, Roy the fugitive—conceivably; but Roy the cold-blooded girl-killer, this she couldn't grasp. Yet there it was. Perhaps MacFaddin already knew, was calling to tell her. Whatever the detective wanted, it could wait.

She went through her mail, reported the credit cards, called Mrs Wing about coming in, and her local deli to have some essentials delivered. And all the time, in the back of her mind, tap-tapping away was the conviction that, come what may, there was one person she must share her awful knowledge with: Kristi's mother, Kim Haggard. And only one person might be able to tell her where the Haggards were estivating: Selina Frampton.

Selina didn't probe. From the sound of it, other matters absorbed her attention. "September?" she said, "Oh Newport most likely. Yes," she confirmed, "September in Newport was always a sacred time for Kim. Quality time. Family time. The one time of year Tad's yachting schedule and the twins' vacations coincided. She'd leave all her causes behind in Toronto and become den mother to her own brood.

"The house? Yes, we went down one year. Out towards The Breakers, you know, the Vanderbilt place. The ocean side of town. In fact, remember the guy with the wife in a coma? Von something. They made a movie. Right across from there. Something to do with trees. High Beeches, that was it. So you're still on his trail? I doubt Kim and Tad would be much help, but keep me posted. Believe you me, I'd like to nail the bastard."

The very next day Annette flew to Providence, Rhode Island, rented a car, and drove to Newport. A patch of swelteringly hot weather, with temperatures in the nineties, had left the Eastern Seaboard gasping. Otherwise the contrast between her previous weekend—in the jungles of Central America—and here in this old New England seaport with its prissy tourist overlay, could hardly have been greater.

In a way Annette didn't mind much whether she saw Kim Haggard or not. But she couldn't not try. She felt she owed that to the family. And calling ahead—even had the number been listed —was out of the question. There are things you can't discuss on the phone. From a purely selfish point of view, Annette needed a break. She knew in her heart of hearts that her life couldn't go on as before, and there was nowhere like a new place for serious thinking about the future.

High Beeches. Cruising those quiet streets heavy with summer greenery, it wasn't long before she found it. The gates in the obscuring brick wall were open, but for some reason—perhaps sudden shyness—she parked in the road outside. At first glimpse, the house had a forbidding aspect: slabs of chiseled, gray stone capped by red-tiled turrets that peeked through the encircling trees, gargoyles and chimneys and odd slit windows and a dark, screened-in porch. The great branch of one of the beeches lay chopped up across the lawn, the leaves of all the trees brown and crinkled on the ocean side. A hurricane had thwacked Rhode Island in July and everywhere its effects were evident.

No vehicles were parked in the driveway, and the front door—to Annette's eyes—might have been sealed up for years. She veered to the left where a concrete path led through a little archway attached to the house, past trashcans to a red door marked SERVICE. Pausing before pushing the bell, she thought she heard music—the rise and fall of an aria—coming from inside. It was a little before four in the afternoon. Pressing a second time, she waited, unsure if the bell worked, then tried pummeling with a fist. A white cat emerged from some bushes to stare. Finally she grabbed a bit of firewood and smote the door with that.

A grating sound caused her to look up: a window opening on the second floor. A woman's head poked out. "Yes, what is it?"

"Oh hi, I'm looking for Mrs Haggard," Annette shouted, embarrassed that she was still holding the log. "I'm Annette Warrender, and I've just flown up from New York, hoping to see her." Getting no response, she added lamely, "Would she be available?"

"What's it about?"

"Well, um, actually it's kind of personal."

The woman let the words hang in the air between them. Then, "Just a minute," she said. It was more like fifteen minutes before Annette heard noises at the door. The woman who opened it was wearing make-up, a green silk blouse and attractive jade earrings.

"Hello. I'm Kim Haggard." Fiftyish, patrician, with a haunted sadness in otherwise kind eyes, dark hair streaked with gray. "I'm sorry. Tell me your name again."

"Annette Warrender. Roy Warrender's first wife. The one before Selina."

She gave Annette a quick, curious look—"Ah yes, poor Roy"— and led the way down a cool, dark corridor into a spacious kitchen. "You don't mind if we sit in here, do you? When it's just the family we don't bother with the rest of the place. It's far too big. Things were so different in our parents day. Now, what can I fix you? Something long and cool I should think."

When they were both sitting with gin and tonics at a table and Annette had taken a good gulp of hers, she felt infinitely better. "It's Roy I came to see you about." She stopped, hating herself for what she was about to say, for troubling this somber woman's mind with such memories. Yet not to say it would surely have been worse.

"I heard he'd disappeared," Kim Haggard encouraged. "Has he turned up again? I wouldn't be surprised. Roy, of all the people I've known, was among the most versatile."

"Well he has, in a way." Annette fumbled for the words, "Yes, it's a long story, but to cut it short, I went looking for him and, well, Roy's dead."

"Oh, you poor dear." Kim Haggard's sympathy reflexes kicked in and she grasped Annette's hand across the table.

"No, no, it's not that," Annette said, withdrawing her hand, then thinking that perhaps she shouldn't have. "We weren't close any more. We hadn't been in touch at all for years. The thing is, what I found out—and I haven't told anybody because I had to see you first—it was Roy who killed your daughter."

To Annette's surprise, Kim Haggard took the news stoically. She got up and splashed more gin into both their glasses before saying anything. And when she did speak it was to ask exactly how Annette had learned about it. Annette explained about Kjelborg—who Kim seemed only vaguely to recall—and Roy's confession to him, and the desperate get-rich-quick scheme, and the cave where Roy died. And when it was all between them on the table, Kim lit a cigarette and blew out a lungful of smoke, and said, "There's only one problem."

Annette couldn't believe her ears. "I'm sorry?" she said, when Kim paused for another deep drag.

"There's only one problem. Yesterday I had a call from Toronto, from the detective in charge of the case." She hunted through some scraps of paper by the phone. "She told me that fresh information had come to light about Kristi's death and that an arrest was imminent."

"But that means—" Annette was stunned. "Detective sergeant MacFaddin, right?"

"I must say, she's incredibly persistent ."

"But—" Annette found herself blushing, as if she'd somehow been caught out, "Did she say who?"

"No, she didn't. And frankly—I hope this won't shock you—I don't care. I wish they'd stop it, all this turning up the earth over Kristi's grave. Let her be. It won't bring her back. I have two other children—twins—the same age as Kristi was when she died. Why should they grow up in the shadow of this tragedy? Why?" As Kim reached out to knock the ash from her cigarette, Annette saw how her hand trembled. She does care a lot, she thought, about something.

"I'm so sorry." Annette stood up. "I shouldn't have come."

"Don't say that. I should be sorry. About Roy. And don't think for a minute he had anything to do with my daughter's death. I'd put that right out of your mind." She leaned back in her chair and looked up at Annette as if seeing her for the first time. "So, his first wife? Sometimes I wonder if I wasn't partly to blame for what happened. With Roy, I mean. I'd no idea how desperate he was."

"How do you mean?"

"To fit in, to be like us, I suppose. The trouble is, he only saw the outside. Well," she rose from the table, "I better do something about dinner. Tad and the twins will be in soon."

"Are they yachtsmen too, the twins?"

"I'm afraid so."

"Afraid?"

"That I'll lose them to the wind and the water, like I lost Tad."

An arrest is imminent. Annette badly wanted to sit in her car and collect her thoughts from where they had scattered after the bombshell so casually tossed out; but Kim Haggard walked out to see her off.

Finding herself on a street that ended at the ocean, she parked and leaned on a railing entwined with pink and white dog roses. Below, on the greenish black rocks, stood two fishermen with rods outthrust. She breathed in the seaweed smell and listened to the mewing cries of gulls and the lazy swell and crash of the sea which stretched to the horizon.

If an arrest was imminent and Roy was dead, then Roy was off the hook. On the other hand, if Roy was guilty and an arrest was imminent, perhaps Roy wasn't dead after all. Or had Mac-Faddin arrested someone entirely innocent? Damn Roy. She wished she'd never set eyes on him.

CHAPTER TWENTY TWO

"Annie darling, oh Annie, Annie, Annie." As soon as Annette heard Colin's preamble on the machine, she knew she was in trouble. This verbal handwringing was reserved for very special chastisement. "The thing of it is, Annie, I'd forgiven you. I'd even shouldered some of the blame. I worried about you, Annie, I really did. How lonely you must have felt without me. Oh Annie, if only you'd waited. Six months, a year. How little must you have considered what *I* was going through. But I never complained, did I? Never used your shoulder to cry on, did I, Annie?"

If only you had, she thought, bracing herself for what was coming. If only you had.

"I can quite see you wanting to take a little holiday. In fact, I wondered why you didn't get away more often, knowing how busy I've become and how impossible it's been to shake free from work to be together more. Harder to understand was your leaving without a word, without a thought for my feelings. But even that, and the moderate expenses you incurred on your trips to Belize and elsewhere, are things I could have—indeed did—overlook. A word of apology or explanation would have sufficed. But to do what you did—what the evidence of my own eyes tells me you did —and expect forgiveness? This is not the Annie I knew and cared for. This is not an Annie I'd want to know. I simply cannot believe that, knowing me as you do, you would expect forgiveness. In fact, were I to extend it, you would have every reason to despise me for doing so.

"I take it then that this is adieu. I shall be leaving London again in a few hours for Mumbai by chartered jet with the maharishi who, incidentally, is failing by the hour. In the meantime, I have informed the building management of your altered situation. Perhaps you'd be good enough to turn over your keys and leave an address with them to which your mail and so on can be forwarded. I'm sad that it had to end like this, but A—"

She sat transfixed. Once or twice her hand twitched toward the phone, but her biceps felt like Jell-O. What was the point anyway? At this hour—midnight in London—if he'd left already, she'd wake up his wife. What had gotten to him, if not her charged expenses? *The evidence of my own eyes.* Evidence of what? She'd known it was time to call it quits. Well, it had happened. Just more abruptly than envisioned.

Pacing the apartment at last she came to a decision, lifted the phone, and dialed.

"Hello?" a voice answered.

"Listen, Jadwiga, it's me. Will you take pity on a poor refugee?"

CHAPTER TWENTY THREE

Several days after Annette transferred her clothes and what little else she could claim as hers from the place on the Upper East Side to Jadwiga's walk-up off Ninth Avenue in the Manhattan district known as Hell's Kitchen, an envelope arrived in the mail. No ordinary-looking envelope, it was of crinkly blue paper and bore the typed address of her former apartment and the stamps of *Republica Argentina*. No return address was given, but the postmark said Buenos Aires, with a date ten days ago.

Slitting along the flap, Annette extracted a sheaf of typed pages. Checking for a signature, she could scarcely believe her eyes. Hardly daring to hope, suspecting perhaps a cruel joke of timing, she double-checked the postmark. She'd been fooled once, she wouldn't fall for it again. Sitting at Jadwiga's kitchen table in the lamplight—though it was the middle of the day—her head in her hands, she read.

My dear Annette,

Where to begin after all this time? And how to thank you? When they told me a woman was looking for me—a gringo and a man with a gun, they said—the last person I thought of was you. Not because I didn't often think of you and the times we had together, but because—after what I did to you—could I blame you for never wanting to see me again? I still don't understand how—or why—you managed to find me. It seemed like another of those make-or-break times in my life when—so richly unde-served—my guardian angel leaned over my shoulder and filled my empty plate to overflowing. At least when I do, eventually, get back on my feet, I'll know who my friends are. Because—be-

lieve your poor old Roy, Annette—I've found out the hard way about my enemies.

Do you remember Kjelborg? Of course you do. Best man and oldest friend—save you—I count him chief among my betrayers. And let me tell you why, because getting it off my chest will make me feel a whole lot better. And right now, Annette, you're the only audience I have that I can trust.

Last spring, I suppose, is as far back as we need go. Though the roots of my tale are nurtured in far older soil. To put it mildly, I was on my uppers. Business had not blossomed. I owed a lot of money, much of it to not very nice, not very patient, people. I had no fallback position. I was, in a word, desperate. And as is the wont of desperados, I conned myself into a line of action that, in my right mind, I'd have scoffed at out of hand.

Let me insert here a smidgeon of background. Ten years ago, in Toronto, the daughter of a family with whom I was very close, was murdered. It was a particularly brutal killing and the culprit, to this day, hasn't been arrested. I myself—because I knew the girl and was near her place at the time—was questioned and briefly detained. You can imagine the trauma. I came near to throwing in the towel. Kjelborg saved me. Without his help I'd have landed myself in the soup good and proper. It was only this past May I discovered—quite by chance—that, in saving me, he had developed a shrewd idea of the identity of the killer, and was living comfortably on the proceeds, if you get my drift.

It was then that greed got the lock on me. I contacted Kjelborg and asked what it would be worth for me to keep my mouth shut. (I wasn't 100% sure of his scam, just knew there was one.) He laughed, pointing out I'd need one helluva lot more than he had access to for the sort of thing I had in mind, i.e. get back on my feet financially. (My debts amounted to a cool half million.) His scam, he said, was low budget, and that was the beauty of it. It kept him and his wife in cornflakes. (She was an invalid, we never met.) Kjelborg said he had a deal going that he'd cut me in on 50/50, that would solve my problem.

He claimed he was onto nothing less than the biggest potential legal dumping ground for hazardous waste in the Western Hemisphere. At a time when governments were desperate for safe nuclear cemeteries, here was one on our very doorstep that hardly needed a spade's worth of digging to be operational. Belize, to me, was a blank, but Kjelborg had spent time there last year researching a book on the Maya, he said, and that's how he'd come across these caves: miles and miles of them, granite, he said, impermeable. So we went into business as Kjelborg & McKenzie. Part of the deal was for Roy Warrender, defaulter, to quit the scene in favor of Calvin McKenzie, entrepreneur.

How Kjelborg must have chortled. He had me twisted around his little finger. I still marvel at the boldness of it all. That the whole thing was a set-up didn't occur to me even when I woke from unconsciousness to water thudding in my ears. Need I describe that treacherous cave? The miracle was I landed where I did, not dashed to pieces in that foaming torrent. A bang on the head and a wrenched shoulder didn't stop me from inching my way out. Only when I saw the car, key in ignition, my passport in the glove compartment, did I suspect. Scrambling back up to the cavern, limestone (and hence porous) I now realized, I found a flashlight artfully arranged by the hole I'd fallen through. The only thing that dump was ever intended to dispose of was yours truly.

After my initial fury, it dawned on me that there was a silver lining. If I wasn't about to become a toxic waste millionaire, at least I was dead and could plan a timely comeback. Studying the map I figured I'd hike from settlement to settlement, cross the mountains at their southern end, and head for the coast. I didn't fancy heading west into Guatemala. I tell you, Annette, 95% of those settlements didn't exist. If it wasn't for an old chiclero I met on the trail that first night, I'd be an archeological site myself now.

This wizened old chicle gum gatherer saved my life. Though we'd hardly a word in common, I've had no better teacher anytime ever. He taught me survival in a hostile environment, yes. But he taught me something about survival that, if I'd learned long ago, might have made my life very different. At first I offered him money. He refused. I became paranoid, convinced he planned to kill and rob me. I was helpless and he surely knew it.

Gradually, as we made our way through jungle, across rivers and over mountains, this feeling of helplessness stayed with me. I began to accept it and wear it like a well-worn garment. And it dawned on me that each one of us, as we make our individual way, is helpless. That anything else is illusory, and to accept this is to liberate mental and physical energy we never dreamed we had. Coming over those mountains I've never known greater hardship, but I've never known greater strength. I soared.

By the same count, in the village where you found me—or didn't—I was equally helpless. Anyone could have handed me over to the man with the gun. But no, they were all refugees, fleeing from the persecution of their Guatemalan overlords. I think they sensed in me a kindred spirit.

Annette! The sight of you after these many moons! It was all I could do not to run and wrap my arms around you, though my straggly beard and weathered mud-stained clothes would have scared the daylights out of you. How well you look. And what a mess I've made since leaving you. When they brought me your bag—because I had to know why you'd come, though it offered no clue—believe me I was of two minds. On the one hand, here was my deliverance, my ticket to the future; on the other: Thou Shalt Not Steal. In the end, I gambled. I was sure you were there for me. Why else would you keep a photo of a gawky kid in Mexico City all those years ago?

Well, help me you did. And now at last I can thank you. The cash I will refund when I can. The charges against your bank you should have no difficulty writing off assuming you declare the card stolen. In case this troubles you, everybody does it.

I'm not where this is coming from, but now that I know where you are, I'll try to keep in touch. Wish me luck in this new life.

Your late, not so great, Roy.

For a long time Annette sat, chin in hands, staring at the pale blue pages with their blur of characters till the lines rose and fell like an ocean swell, driving her giddy. So Colin thought she'd given someone her credit card. Well, that solved that one. And Roy likely maxed it out. The relief she felt that Roy was alive was somewhat eclipsed by anger and bafflement at the man who'd convinced her otherwise. What was Kjelborg playing at? And what on earth reason could he have for pinning on Roy this terrible murder? If he was wrong on the first count, was he wrong on the second? Yes, there might be a very good reason. She walked into the living room and, sitting down on Jadwiga's maroon velvet couch, pulled the phone towards her.

Soon the persuasive inflections of Edinburgh seeped from the instrument and Annette found herself the object of a mild scolding. MacFaddin had tried a half dozen times to reach her. "I had it in mind to pick your brains on a couple of points, but no matter, we were able to go ahead anyway. You'll be interested to hear that, thanks in no small part to you, there's been an arrest in the Kristi Aranda case."

Annette gulped, "You mean you know who did it? You've got him?"

"I just said, an arrest."

"Can you tell me?"

"Soren Gustavus Kjelborg." Perhaps because of the dazed silence at the end of the line, she added, "Surprise?"

"But he's in Guatemala. I was with him."

"He's in the Don Jail, down the road from here. We picked him up on Wednesday. We were waiting for him. So far he's charged with one count of entering the country under an assumed name, and one count of attempted kidnapping with a view to murder. Detective Ruiz obtained a deposition from the boatman he hired to deep six you. To put it bluntly."

"Oh my god," Annette murmured, more to herself than to Toronto. "It never even occurred to me. *Kjelborg.* An hour ago, ten minutes ago, I wouldn't have believed you. Can I read you something?" She read out Roy's letter in its entirety.

"Now I'm the dumbfounded one." MacFaddin seemed impressed, bordering on gleeful. "That's precisely what I needed. Annette, you're invaluable."

"So Roy's out of the picture?"

"Didn't I tell you that when we first met?"

"Funny. Kristi's mother said the same thing. I saw her last weekend. Put it right out of your mind, she said." She explained about her time with Kjelborg at the Hotel del Norte, and her subsequent visit to Kim Haggard in Newport.

"Yes," said MacFaddin, "I've a hunch she's always suspected the truth. It's not going to be easy. Ah well," she sighed, "a policeman's lot, you know."

An hour later the phone rang in Jadwiga's living room. Toronto was calling back. "I must have mislaid my thinking cap when we were talking just now, Annette. Is there any way we could entice you up here?" Sensing hesitation, she added, "I think it might be crucial."

CHAPTER TWENTY FOUR

Life without Colin—Annette had had no further word and imagined him in India with his maharishi—was life without cash. That was the immediate difference. As luck would have it, Jadwiga was leaving to visit relatives in Poland and had asked Annette to step into her shoes at the guichet for the time she'd be gone. Breathing space to look for a job. It was awkward to have to tell Flora Mac-Faddin that she couldn't afford a trip to Toronto.

The detective sergeant, it became clear, was not taking no for an answer. For the second time in a month she flew north above the sprawling forests, rivers, lakes and towns of upstate New York, and descended over the wind-scuffed waters of Lake Ontario. Only this time Toronto was footing the bill.

Tea and biscuits had been ritually produced, small talk exchanged. The time had come for MacFaddin to clear her throat and, leaning her forearms on that still uncluttered desk, to say, "Frankly, Annette, we're in a bit of a bind. Friend Kjelborg's mouth is very firmly shut. Not a peep. Not his name, nothing. Not even what he takes in his tea."

"As far as I know he's a coffee person."

"Your letter from Warrender," she touched it where it lay between them, "confirms everything I'm beginning to suspect. Our man's a goldmine, I'm convinced, if we could only get him started."

"Who's he blackmailing, do you think?"

"Between you and me and the teapot, I've had my suspicions all along."

THE FIRST WIFE'S TALE

Annette waited, but MacFaddin was tightlipped. "I don't quite see how I can help."

"Bringing the two of you together may do it. Shock tactics. The one he thought he'd disposed of."

"I still find that hard to fathom."

"Protecting his source of income. You knew too much. Warrender ditto." She patted the letter. "You knew about the wife?"

"No. I didn't know he was married." She felt bleak. "OK," she nodded. "OK."

Whipping through downtown Toronto in the back of an unmarked squad car, she told herself over and over that the man she was on her way to see deserved whatever was coming to him. Yet intruding around the edges was the memory of their time together not so long ago on the balcony at the Hotel del Norte. It didn't add up.

If she'd envisaged a confrontation through prison bars, Annette was wrong. Kjelborg was seated on one side of a square table in a room with the feel of a small institutional cafeteria from which most of the furniture had been removed. He was flanked by two guards. Armed guards stood at each exit. Across from him sat the detective sergeant, cool in a summer suit. As she walked in, summoned by a guard, Kjelborg looked up. It was his eyebrows gave him away. It seemed to Annette that they jerked convulsively. His face in the tube lighting, haggard and drained of color, registered nothing. Obscenely, she found herself smiling.

"Soren Adolphus Kjelborg," intoned MacFaddin in the manner of a judge passing sentence, "the charges against you include the attempted murder of Annette Shaheen Warrender on the seventh of September last, and the attempted murder of Roy-lance Calvin Warrender on or about the seventh day of August of the same year." At the second *attempted* Kjelborg visibly stiffened and stole a glance at the door as if Roy might also walk through it. "You know your rights," MacFaddin concluded. "If I were you I'd get myself a lawyer."

Kjelborg's eyes roamed the ceiling. "I guess I'll do that," he said.

"I'll see you back here at five o'clock. That should be time enough." As Kjelborg was escorted from the room, she gathered up her files. "Well, well, well," she nodded at Annette after the door closed behind him.

Annette felt sick to her stomach. For an awful moment, she thought she'd throw up.

In the early afternoon of the following day the call that Annette had been waiting for came through. She was in the dining room at the Royal York—where she'd gone for a late lunch—when she heard herself paged over the intercom.

"It's a grisly business," MacFaddin's voice was strained, different, "and about as twisted as a corkscrew, but I think we've finally got it straightened out. There's no pressing reason for us to keep you here, but I think you should know where things stand." She sounded grim.

On her way back to her room Annette passed the bar where she'd rendezvoused with Kjelborg. She shuddered at the thought of the declaration of love he had proffered there, and recalled with horror the night on the upstairs balcony of the Hotel del Norte. How close she'd come—despite Selina's warning—to allowing herself to be added to his list of conquests. How convincingly he'd lied, all the time knowing precisely what had happened.

Annette walked the ten blocks to Police Headquarters. It was a perfect day, not too hot, the sky above the tall buildings as blue and innocent as painted porcelain. Very still, expectant, the sort of day that made you doubt the power of evil. Little clouds, like fluffed up white of egg, were faintly underscored with gray. She gave her name to the duty officer in the lobby and was asked to wait, the detective sergeant would be with her as soon as possible. Annette took in the people around her and through the plate glass windows, in the plaza and street beyond. The late September sunshine threw everything into relief and she felt as if she'd spent half her life away somewhere, out of it, and was just now resuming her place among the to-ing and fro-ing of the humdrum human race. Then Flora MacFaddin was greeting her from the far side of some mental abyss.

Up in the fourth floor office, with the door closed, the two women faced each other across the desk, the one alert with expectation, the other wrapped in a tangle of gloom. "It's weird," said the detective, "for ten years I've worried away at this case like a terrier at a rabbit hole. I've lived for the day when the wee beast I'm after is wriggling between my jaws. But it's never quite the way you think it's going to be, is it? Plain truth has a way of disappointing."

A tap on the door brought the inevitable tea tray. MacFaddin did the honors. "First off I should thank you for providing just the touch of oil needed to get the locomotive moving," she said. "Without that we'd still be sitting in the shed. As to the long and the short of it, here goes: friend Kjelborg spills the beans on the Kristi Aranda murder and in return the Law casts an indulgent eye on his manifold sins and wickednesses. It's the devil's game, Annette, make no mistake about it."

"He's cooperating?"

"Oh yes. We were up till the wee hours. And most of today's been spent sussing his story out. So far, touch wood, it holds up. In all important aspects." She proffered the Digestives with their taint of Colin. "I wonder if the best approach wouldn't be for me to recap his tale more or less the way he told it?" She buzzed the intercom. "No calls please, Maureen, for the time being. The usual exceptions."

Lifting a typescript dossier from a drawer, she scanned it briefly, put it aside and leaned back. "A delightful story. The marriage of lust and greed. And they might have gotten away with it, had you not stumbled on the scene. Let's go back ten years to the Haggards, Kim and Tad. Wealthy, popular, society people. Kim a few years older than her husband. Her second marriage. Twins, eight years old. A daughter, Kristi, by her first husband, a Spanish diplomat, deceased; eighteen, sports-loving, party-going, spending her summer after high school crewing on her step-father's yacht in the Mediterranean where she meets, and falls in love with, a strapping, molten-eyed Moroccan laddie.

"Into this enchanted world Kjelborg has a peephole thanks to his old pal, Roy Warrender, charity fund-raiser par excellence and, as such, received into the Forest Hill heart of the Haggard family, though not so much friend as courtier. A distinction he perhaps fails to grasp.

"Then, in the late fall of the year, disaster strikes. Kristi is found strangled in the apartment she has only weeks before moved into. The person who finds her, at eight o'clock that evening, is the Moroccan boyfriend—whom she was expecting and to whom a plane ticket had been sent. Her door is off the latch, he says. He walks in. Oh yeah? say the cops. Luckily for him, his plane is hours late. Kristi, the experts say, has been dead since lunchtime. Arrested, he's reluctantly released, and skedaddles back to France. The police are baffled. Interviews with all Kristi's friends—she has many—are scheduled, fingerprints taken. Suddenly, nothing is obvious.

"Warrender had confessed to being near Kristi's place at the time of her death, visiting an artist who did work for his office; said he even considered stopping by to suggest a bite. He'd done it before. Figured it might look suspicious if he'd been seen and not come forward. But with the boyfriend off the hook, he was not only called back for further questioning, but detained. Bail was set and was met—somewhat to the chagrin of the Law—by Kristi's own family. The case against him collapsed.

"Kjelborg, during this period, was living in Minnesota, working in a library, and had recently learned that his wife of one year had diseased kidneys. At the time of Warrender's arrest, he received a call from Warrender's wife, Selina, begging him to come to Toronto. Roy, she said, was having some sort of breakdown. She couldn't cope.

"Warrender and Kjelborg were buddies from their college days, as I'm sure you know. Kjelborg responded. Here, for the first time, he says, he heard the ins and outs of the Kristi murder. Warrender, fresh from a police cell, was a blubbering wreck, convinced he was being made the scapegoat in a high profile murder. According to Kjelborg, he'd always had a chip on his shoulder. At his lowest ebb, he told him that he'd rather just confess and have done with it. His reputation was in tatters. He'd nothing left to live for.

"Gradually Kjelborg nursed his friend back from the brink. And in doing so, found himself wrestling with the conundrum posed by the case. With the boyfriend out of the running, at first glance he figured that one candidate stood head and shoulders above the rest. The stepfather."

"My feeling too," said Annette.

MacFaddin might not have heard. "So Kjelborg took a long, hard look at Tad Haggard. He maintains, by the way, that the scam that eventually developed was not, at that point, in his mind. Personally, I hae me doots—he was in dire need of funds for his wife's treatment—but that's between him and his maker and there's not a lot we can do about it. Tad Haggard had an alibi. He was on his yacht in Bermuda. But he was alone on his yacht. With careful planning it is logistically conceivable that he flew to Toronto, committed the crime, and flew back to Hamilton.

"Assuming that's what happened, the next question Kjelborg asked himself was, Why? Were Kristi and her stepfather having an affair? Was it the one-sided obsession of an older man? Had she been molested, raped even, and threatened not to tell. Kjelborg flew to Nice—we've confirmed this—tracked down the Moroccan boyfriend who was studying there, and satisfied himself in an ostensibly casual chat that Tad had a reputation *avec les jeunes filles*. The boyfriend also revealed that his round trip ticket to Toronto was mailed to him direct from a travel agent and that, while Kristi had promised it, there was no indication that it actually came from her.

"Was it a set-up? Was it possible that Tad had killed Kristi because she was pregnant with his child, then set up the boyfriend to take the rap? The evidence was circumstantial. The family strenuously objected to a full-scale post mortem, the body had been cremated. But for Kjelborg, it was enough.

"When he further discovered—largely hearsay he admits—that Tad's vaunted wealth from family mining interests had dwindled spectacularly and he was largely dependent on his wife's resources to support his yachting, Kjelborg was, as they say, ready to rest his case. He sat down and wrote—not to Tad, but shrewdly to Kim. He didn't ask for much, just five grand U.S. to be deposited in the bank on the third Wednesday of each month. The name he chose for himself was Tom Barton, and for his organization, The Green Earth Society. She took it as a tax write-off. Kjelborg found himself with a modest income for life, at least for Kim Haggard's life.

"Tad never suspected. For ten years—that's six hundred thousand smackeroos—everything rolled smoothly along.

"According to Kjelborg, the trouble started when Warrender 'got religion'. In the years since Kristi's death things had not gone well for Roy. His magic touch deserted him. His marriage soured. His business failed. Debts mounted. Girlfriends came and went. Even his son spurned him. Remember, this is Kjelborg talking. Finally, in the spring of this year, the two old friends met—a rare reunion—on one of Kjelborg's Toronto visits. Warrender, a few over the eight, blubbers that he's something on his conscience he's convinced all his ill fortune stems from. He needs to unload. He's met this girl—some kind of divinity student—and wants to confess the error of his ways and do penance. At last he gets it out. It's Kristi, he tells Kjelborg. He killed her."

Annette nodded. "That's the version I heard."

"Lordy lor, here we go again, is how Kjelborg described his reaction. But, like the Ancient Mariner, Warrender insisted. Back in Kjelborg's hotel room, his friend, cold sober, is taking him step by step through what happened that day in that Queen Street West walkup. He believed him."

"More to the point, can you believe Kjelborg?"

"Fair question," MacFaddin acquiesced. "I don't know how much detail he went into with you—about Warrender's confession I mean, for lack of a better word?"

"It sounded like jacket copy off a bodice ripper, the little I heard."

MacFaddin pressed her fingers to her lips. "Remember my telling you there was evidence at the crime scene that only the killer could know about? Some of that came up in what Warrender told Kjelborg."

"*Yes*," Annette pounced, "*that only the killer could know about*. Well, Kjelborg apparently knew, and you've only his word that Roy told him."

"We've had people in Minneapolis since Wednesday checking out Kjelborg's movements. We can't place him in Toronto the day of Kristi's murder. He's firmly in Edina."

"You've had Roy in your sights all along," Annette accused bitterly. "Kjelborg's framed him and you're going along."

"Not so. True, I have had someone in my sights, but not Warrender. The step-father, Tad Haggard. You have to be on very firm ground in this town before you mess with a wealthy socialite."

"As opposed to a pathetic parvenu like Roy."

MacFaddin ignored the barb. "To go on with Kjelborg's account: last spring, as I said, he panicked when Roy came to him. Saw his livelihood going belly-up. He really does have a wife and she is hooked up to a dialysis machine. Overnight, he said, he came up with the Belize toxic waste scheme idea, and Warrender leapt at it. Gone was the saintly martyr prepared to immolate himself on the flames of his conscience. Enter the swashbuckling privateer.

"Kjelborg had been in Belize last year researching a book and had almost fallen through that bottomless hole himself. He managed to spirit Roy out of Canada and the clutches of his creditors, then went to work on his plan. With an Ottawa number and a few sheets of masthead stationery, *Kjelborg & McKenzie* was in business. He fancied he'd be sitting pretty for the rest of Kim Haggard's natural life. You were the wild card he didn't reckon on."

The phone buzzed. MacFaddin picked up. From the pitch of her voice Annette guessed it was her superior. "Yes, Sir. Yes, yes. Precisely. Not at all, Sir. Right away. Excellent. Fine. I'll do that." Replacing the receiver she looked at Annette with something like triumph in her eyes. "Well, we're in business. We don't go in for plea-bargaining here to quite the extent you do down south, but there's ways and means, with clearance from the top. That's what that was about."

Annette stared incredulously at her, fingers tight around the arms of her chair. "I don't believe this."

"Without Kjelborg's testimony a murderer walks."

"It's only hearsay. I can't believe a judge would allow it. Roy was right. He's easy meat. He's no one to speak for him."

"Except himself." From a drawer of her desk Flora Mac-Faddin lifted a small tape recorder. "Perhaps I should have used this earlier. I'd have like to spare you." She touched a button and the whoosh of static flooded the small room.

Annette leaned closer. "I was in the neighborhood"—a man was speaking—"It was lunchtime. I couldn't get her out of my mind. I'd been up there to see her the week before and she told me never to come again. All the same, she let me in. She was expecting someone any minute, she said pointedly, some guy she'd met over the summer in France. I got the message, said I wouldn't stay. Just one kiss."

More static, like cars passing in the distance, the occasional beep. Annette's heart thudded dangerously. She was sweating. Then a second voice prompted, "Take your time."

"I don't know what got into me. It was when she turned away, the look on her face. Sort of disgust, like I was a bad smell in that turned-up patrician little nose of hers. I ripped off my scarf and caught her round the neck and tugged and tugged. There was a demon in me. I dragged her to the bed and ripped her clothes a bit and left the door off the latch so they'd think it was him. They always go for the lover.

"I don't know how I made it back to the office, must have walked all the way. It was someone else had done that, not me. Later, going home, I couldn't find my scarf. Had I left it round her neck, dropped it on the street, on the stairs. I panicked. My mind was blank. It was a present from Selina. My poppy too. Gone. When they didn't buy the lover bit, I freaked out."

MacFaddin clicked off the machine. "When the tenant in Apartment One died a few weeks ago—deaf and dumb she was, and gaga into the bargain, poor soul—the super came across a men's silk scarf in cleaning out her place, recalled the case and brought it to our attention. The old thing probably picked it up on the stairs that afternoon. I have it here."

It was all Annette could do to force herself to look at the clear plastic bag the detective laid before her on the desk. "See there, the poppy," she pointed. "It was Remembrance Day and they were selling them on the street. Those hairs—you can just make them out—we've had them tested. Kristi's. Now look at this." She produced an envelope from a drawer and extracted a photo. "Kristi's neck. See that mark. It's a bruise. Her killer's poppy got caught up in his scarf. It caused that. It puzzled the heck out of us."

STOP! Annette wanted to yell. Stop this torture. Hunched in horrified concentration, she watched tongue-tied as MacFaddin stowed away the tape recorder. "Just an old blackmailer's insurance policy."

"Can you put someone on trial whose not here?" Annette managed.

"No, but sooner or later they give themselves away. And I'll be waiting. The cat at the mouse hole. Tell me, Annette," the frank green eyes drilled into her, "if it ever came to it, would you be willing to take the stand against him? To verify his voice, for instance, if it comes to that?"

She thought a moment, leaned her head into her hands and sobbed freely. The detective watched for a while, then reached for a box of Kleenex. "Would you let me know if you hear from him again?"

Annette had no words left. She sat, helpless. MacFaddin smiled. "Well, if you ever change your mind."

POSTSCRIPT

It was the last day of October, Halloween, the day Jadwiga was due back from Europe. Annette planned a little surprise. She had squirted fake cobwebs around the living room and hung up paper witches and skull-and-crossbones with abandon, and was reading the hand-lettered label on a plastic baggie she'd picked up in Belize: SACRED INSCENCE TO PROTECT YOU AND YOUR HOUSE AWAY FROM BAD SPIRITS BAD LUCK AND DISASTORS. Perfect. Tipping a little into a saucer in the kitchen, she lit a match to it. At that exact moment the intercom buzzed. Surely way too soon for Jadwiga.

"Yes?" She hit the TALK button then released it, unsure who was supposed to talk: herself, the person downstairs or perhaps both. Jadwiga had warned her about kids yelling obscenities. Hearing nothing, she pressed again and the word, Warrender, crackled in her ears. Reflexively hitting the DOOR button, she panicked. Already she heard the plod, plod, plod of ascending feet. Her hand went to her neck, thoughts of Kristi racing through her mind. She turned the Medeco cylinder, set the chain and waited. The footfall reached the fourth floor and stopped.

Gingerly, lest the slightest sound give her away, Annette lifted the flap of the peephole. Such a sweat was she in, that the glass at once fogged up. The steps now moved towards her along the hall. In front of her door they stopped. She could see nothing. A light tap-tapping petrified her. Easing the flap down, she tensed expectantly.

"Annette?"

She bent her head, wondering.

Louder: "Annette?"

The chain rattled off its hook. "My god," she gasped, "Shane!"

"Like, I escaped." In his chain-encrusted boots, ripped black jeans and MEGADEATH T-shirt, he looked like he'd been rolling in the dust. His face, in its mane of hair, gave off a dirty pallor. Dark shadows ringed his eyes. "They said you'd moved."

They faced each other awkwardly. "Well, come on in."

He took in the exotic wallpaper, the piles of plump pillows, the mirrors, the cobwebs, the maroon velvet couch, and—Jadwiga's thrift shop stab at the Turkish harem look—the broken hookah pipe. He sniffed appreciatively at the incense billowing from the kitchen. "Yeah, pretty much what I figured. One problem."

"What?"

"Money."

"That makes two of us."

He didn't get it. "I shouldn't think you'd be cheap."

The penny dropped. "Damn right," she said. "Know what? I priced myself right out of the market. I'm in movies now." (Well, approximately.)

"Shit," he sounded impressed.

"Sit down, I'll fix us something to eat."

When she emerged from the kitchen with turkey sandwiches and a Coke, Shane was fast asleep on the couch. Beside him on the floor was a much folded and grubby envelope. Keeping an eye on the boy, Annette picked it up and knew it was from Roy. The stamps, like medals on a chest no two alike, were a father's touch. *Republica de Paraguay.*

Dear old son, she read, *this is to keep you posted on the state of play hereabouts. Things being what they are and life moving at the pace it does down here, I'm a little pressed to meet our fall deadline. In fact, don't look for me till spring or summer. That's a promise. We'll have good times together, son o' mine, make no mistake about it. Lots of prospects in this neck o' the woods for the likes of you and me. Meanwhile hang in there and don't do anything I wouldn't do. Hasta luego! Your old dad Roy who— believe it or not—loves you dearly.*

Looking at Shane stretched out on the couch, Annette couldn't help thinking of a skinny boy in Mexico City a long, long time ago. A boy whose photo she'd taken and he'd stuck, forgotten, in a Spanish phrasebook. Tiptoeing to the bedroom, she picked up the phone and trembled at what she was about to do.

Later, fed, washed and wrapped in an old flannel bathrobe, he sat on the couch. "I called your mom," she said.

"Man!" he cried accusingly, "she'll send me back to the Buck."

"No, she promised."

"Yeah?" He didn't seem convinced.

"She's glad you're here and safe, and says you can stay if we can find a school for you and you don't make trouble." Far from raising objections, Selina had at once volunteered all necessary funds if only Annette would take care of things. "What do you say to that?"

"OK," he ventured after a pause, "I guess. When Dad comes, I can crash with him."

Thinking back later to that moment on Jadwiga's couch, to that blank, hopeless young face beside her, Annette knew it was then she first felt scorn for Roy. Pure scorn. Strange it had taken so long.

The very next morning Annette placed a call to Toronto. She had thought things over she told Detective sergeant MacFaddin, and was now ready and willing to cooperate with the department in the Kristi Aranda investigation. Within a week, MacFaddin had set her trap. And a few days before Christmas, Roy sprang it.

Oddly enough it was Colin who became the lynchpin of the scheme, after the detective undertook the delicate task of enlightening him as to exactly what had occurred over that summer of suspicion. Not that Annette wanted to set the clock back. She didn't. She liked herself a whole lot better now. But Colin was vital to the success of the plan, and Colin—in the deft hands of Flora MacFaddin—proved play dough.

Once he agreed to reactivate Annette's credit card—and assurances had criss-crossed the Atlantic absolving him from consequences—the stage was set. In cahoots with the serious fraud department of a bank not averse to nailing the thief of their earlier loss, MacFaddin settled down to wait. Two of the personality traits she'd observed in Warrender left her confident that the ploy would work. First, given his vanity-driven self delusion, she judged him entirely capable of believing that Annette wanted to help him. Second, his need for cash to fuel his taste in lifestyles might tempt him to risk continuing using her card. Conceivably, the news that he was wanted on a murder charge hadn't caught up with him.

The first nibble came in Mexico City: a florist. Charged: a dozen red roses. A transaction immediately flagged by the bank. Though the first Annette knew about it was a call from a doorman at her previous address about a flower delivery. The message, unsigned, read: FOR AULD LANG SYNE. Colin? Unlikely.

"He's dipped in a pinky and it tastes good," MacFaddin told her, "and now he's lapping it up. He's gone ahead and charged a car rental. It's going to be a waiting game. Extradition from that part of the world can be tricky."

Three days later Annette heard again from Toronto. "The guy has chutzpah, I'll give him that. Last night he crossed into Arizona from Nogales. Faked ID. Seems unbelievable, but indications are he's headed for a rendezvous with his son. I suppose there's no reason for him to think Shane's anywhere but at Buckhaven. He'll get a nasty surprise."

Annette intimated nothing of this to Shane on his return from school, dreading the moment, perhaps soon, when she'd have to break the news of Roy's arrest.

The call came two days later, from Colorado. The detective sergeant had to struggle to maintain a professional mien. At Buckhaven she'd had the satisfaction of personally reading to a dumbfounded Warrender the charges against him, eleven years, one month and thirteen days after Kristi's murder. "The best Christmas present I could ever have given myself," she told Annette.

The trial, in the spring, was the talk of Toronto. For his evidence, which the jury credited for the speed and unanimity of their verdict, Kjelborg's sentence was partially reduced. He was charged with perverting the course of justice, blackmail and two counts of attempted murder. Not once during the proceedings—it was noted in the local papers—did the two old friends meet each other's gaze. To Annette's considerable relief, she was not called to the stand.

At his sentencing, Roy's only request to the judge was to be allowed to meet privately with his son. What transpired at that encounter—which took place in the maximum security area of the Don Jail—is not generally known. Annette never asked. She noted however that on Shane's return to New York he retired his MEGADEATH T-shirt.

THE END

J N CATANACH

This is a work of fiction. Names, characters, places, events and incidents are either the products of the author's imagination, or used in a fictitious manner. Any resemblance to actual persons, living or dead, or to actual events, is coincidental.

J N CATANACH

J N CATANACH

Mysteries by J N Catanach:

WHITE IS THE COLOR OF DEATH

BRIDEPRICE

THE LAST RITE OF HUGO T

LULLABY FOR THE DEAD

GUNNING POINT ROAD

THE SELLING OF BRIGHT IQUO

Co-written as Paul Amber:
THE CORPSE IN CUYLER'S ALLEY

THE FIRST WIFE'S TALE

J N CATANACH

Made in United States
North Haven, CT
18 August 2022

22877648R00136